THE SIEGE
IN THE
ROOM

THE SIEGE
IN THE
ROOM

THREE NOVELLAS

MIQUEL BAUÇÀ

TRANSLATED AND WITH
AN INTRODUCTION BY
MARTHA TENNENT

DALKEY ARCHIVE PRESS
CHAMPAIGN / DUBLIN / LONDON

Originally published in Catalan as *Carrer Marsala*, 1985, and *El vellard; L'escarcellera*, 1992, by Grup Editorial 62, Barcelona.
Carrer Marsala
© Grup Editorial 62, S.L.U., Editorial Empúries, 1985
Peu de la Creu, 4, 08001 Barcelona
www.grup62.cat
El vellard; L'escarcellera
© Grup Editorial 62, S.L.U., Editorial Empúries, 1992
Peu de la Creu, 4, 08001 Barcelona
www.grup62.cat

Translation and introduction copyright © 2012 by Martha Tennent
First edition, 2012

Library of Congress Cataloging-in-Publication Data

Bauçà, Miquel.
[Novels. English. Selections]
The siege in the room / Miquel Bauçà ; translated and with an introduction by Martha Tennent. -- 1st ed.
    p. cm.
"Originally published in Catalan as Carrer Marsala, 1985, and, El vellard; L'escarcellera, 1992, by Grup editorial 62, Barcelona."
ISBN 978-1-56478-770-5 (pbk. : acid-free paper) -- ISBN 978-1-56478-731-6 (cloth : acid-free paper)
1. Bauçà, Miquel--Translations into English. I. Tennent, Martha. II. Title.
PC3942.12.A8A2 2012
849'.9354--dc23
                                2012006982

Partially funded by a grant from the Illinois Arts Council, a state agency

institut
ramon llull
Catalan Language and Culture

The Catalan Literature Series is published in cooperation with the Institut Ramon Llull, a public consortium responsible for the promotion of Catalan language and culture abroad.

www.dalkeyarchive.com

Cover: design and composition by Sarah French

Printed on permanent/durable acid-free paper and bound in the United States of America

CONTENTS

Translator's Introduction

Who was Bauçà?

Even within Catalan literary circles Miquel Bauçà (1940–2005) is something of a minor writer turned cult figure. Born in Felanitx, Mallorca, he has garnered a growing reputation among Catalan literati as an experimental poet and fiction writer. He began as a realist and ended his life as perhaps the most radical stylist, iconoclast, and visionary in Catalan literature.

Bauçà grew up on a farm in Mallorca in the squalid, post-civil war years of the Franco dictatorship. His first experience of running water, seeing a piano, and wearing underwear came when he was sent at the age of twelve as a boarding student to a religious seminary in Palma de Mallorca—"the Capital"—shortly before his mother's death. After graduating from the seminary and doing his military service, he settled in Barcelona, where he attended the university, married, and had a daughter. Here he began a bohemian life as a writer, eking out a living first by giving Catalan lessons and doing archival work for a publishing house and later by passing state exams to teach at a secondary school.

Bauçà won his first literary prize (the Salvat-Papasseit) at age twenty-one for his collection of poems, *Una bella història* (A Beautiful Story, 1962), and his poetry immediately attracted the attention of a small group of young writers. Six other collections of poetry followed. His short book of epigrammatic poems, *Notes i comentaris* (Notes and Commentaries)—winner of the 1974 Vicent Andrés Estellés Prize—marked the tendency for all of his future poetry: his penchant for writing disconcerting poems—often ironic and cynical—that alternate between his uncompromising commentaries on the human condition (loneliness, hope, death, sensuality), quotidian matters (hygiene, technology, telephones, city life), and philosophical concerns. Poem number 38 reads, prophetically:

> A nervous castaway doesn't know
> the topography of the soul.

He wrote five other collections of poems—lyric poems "filled with chaos and confusion . . . [with] an aristocratic taste for language," as one critic put it—before moving to the prose works that are translated here: *Carrer Marsala* (1985) and *The Old Man / The Warden* (published together in 1992). Perhaps Bauçà's best-known work is *El Canvi* (The Change, 1998), a monumental, unclassifiable work of mixed genres organized into an extravagant dictionary. The last period of his life was devoted exclusively to poetry, the alphabetically organized "essays" written in heptasyllabic verses that formed his dictionaries: *Els estats de connivència* (Collusive States, 2001), *Els somnis* (Dreams, 2003), and his posthumous works, *Rudiments de saviesa* (Rudiments of Wisdom, 2005) and *Certituds immediates* (Immediate Certainties, 2007).

Carrer Marsala captured the attention of the wider public and was met with critical acclaim (it received the City of Barcelona and the Cavall Verd literary awards), though the writer continued to refuse interviews and to resist the lure of the literary establishment. Critics placed his work in the line of European experimental writers such as Robert Walser, Dino Buzzati, and Franz Kafka (though he could equally have been compared to Thomas Bernhard for his unapologetically obsessive vitriol), an anomaly among his Catalan peers. Bauçà had certainly received a good education at the seminary and the university, where he read the classics; yet he was, by all accounts, *not* a reader. If Bauçà chose not to read—fearing external "contamination" of his work, as he put it—was his style a reflection of some literary mutation, so to speak? Bauçà did, in any event, own a large collection of dictionaries in several languages, and these fed his vast vocabulary.

The three short novels translated here showcase Bauçà's untrammeled, manic imagination and a linguistic prowess that allowed him to mold the Catalan language to the point, some say, that it seemed almost foreign. *Carrer Marsala, The Old Man,* and *The Warden* unfold in an oneiric, surreal atmosphere of brutal worlds that seem to have become unhinged from discernible reference points, where language has almost supplanted material reality and external facts cannot be trusted. Although these novels retain elements that could be termed realistic, there is no effort to convey the sense of plausibility normally found in fantastic literature. The descriptions of the narrators' thoughts and activities are rendered in a manner that allows in the reader a response similar to that of reading Beckett or Kafka, but here the struggle plays out primarily in the landscape of the narrators' minds. Through them, Bauçà offers us his personal sense of the moral degradation and mediocrity of late twentieth-century Catalan society, the precariousness and anguish of existence, and his view of life as an illness devoid of meaning, a delicate balance between madness and the quotidian drudgery necessary for survival.

The iconic status that Bauçà came to hold among certain Catalan literati would perhaps have caused him to sneer, for above all he wished to be an anonymous, invisible writer. The relative obscurity of his work went hand in hand with his self-imposed ostracism (in a letter written in 1995 he referred to himself as "an apartment hermit") in the tradition of literary exiles such as J. D. Salinger or Thomas Pynchon.

Bauçà's troubled life and character—he suffered from alcoholism and schizophrenia—his provocative writing and his eccentricity (which ranged from a penchant for getting into bed with his acquaintances, male and female, to his fascination with cemeteries or showing up unannounced and drunk on friends' doorsteps, only to retreat into exile for lengthy periods) contributed to the *poète maudit* mystique that enveloped his persona and literary activity, although he would no doubt have objected to this characterization as being too "Parisian."

Many of Bauçà's personal neuroses figure in his novels: his admiration for the United States (he often stated that he wished he'd been born there), his scrupulous hygienic routines, his fixation on sex, religion, smoking, popping pills, and examining himself in the mirror. Obsessive yet lucid, this staunchly Catalan-nationalist (Bauçà referred to Spanish as the "enemy language") eschewed most personal contacts in the last period of his life, refused to accept literary prizes, including the one for *Carrer Marsala*, and communicated with the outside world via his post-office box—though occasionally he would agree to personal encounters at the Estudiantil bar near the University of Barcelona, which he patronized for forty years.

In the zealously guarded private world of his bookless apartment in the Eixample district of Barcelona, Bauçà, a skilled carpenter, built a desk that wrapped around the room and installed tracks that allowed his chair to travel from one side to the other. Here he pounded away on his electric typewriter with its continuous scroll of paper, à la Jack Kerouac.

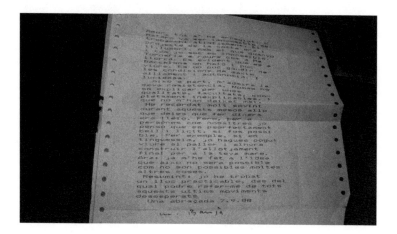

While writing *Carrer Marsala* (*carrer* is Catalan for street), Bauçà often visited his friend and fellow writer Jordi Coca, who lived on the short, eponymous street in Barcelona's Poblenou neighborhood. Bauçà would arrive unannounced, sometimes staying for several days, during which time Coca helped him edit his work. Bauçà would hand him a pair of scissors with the directive: "cut anything you don't understand," something for which readers—confronted with the cryptic quality of the present, expurgated novel—will no doubt be grateful. The actual street, Marsala, never appears in the novel; though one might assume that the title refers to the narrator's address, Bauçà intended it as a dedication to his friend.

Miquel Bauçà (left) and Jordi Coca

Despite being a controversial figure—he has been variously labeled misogynist, racist, and homophobic and was known to harbor a marked distaste for Parisians, weathermen, actors, singers, Germans, novelists, and neighbors in general—the few acquaintances who gained access to him recall him as having an electrifying presence and a basically decent nature. Bauçà's longtime intermittent partner, Amor Estadella, described him as complicated and destructive, intense yet caring, seductive and provocative. He talked often about committing suicide, which he believed should be a legally sanctioned right, and suggested they put an end to their lives.

A letter dated September 7, 1988, written to Estadella upon his return to Barcelona after several years with her in the hamlet of

Toralla in the Catalan Pyrenees, tells of his inner disposition vis-à-vis life and living arrangements:

> It's evident that Barcelona is where I can and must live.
> It's where I can enjoy the greatest isolation and autonomy.
> And lucidity.

From then on, Bauçà became increasingly reclusive, more and more the "apartment hermit" who compulsively wrote those heptasyllabic entries for his colossal poetic dictionaries.

Miquel Bauçà and Amor Estadella, ca. 1974

He died alone in his apartment, sometime around Christmas Day, 2004. The exact date is unknown, a fitting end for the invisible poet, as he was sometimes called. Bauçà, who had written that nothing could compare to the truth contained in dreams, who had devoted an entire book of poems to the subject and believed firmly that "dreams should . . . / . . . free us from our miserable state," had followed to the end Conrad's dictum that "We live as we dream—alone."

*

One could perhaps question the reasons for translating into English a "minor" writer who wrote in a "minor" language, all the more so if we consider that English is generally unreceptive to literary translation. Only a very small number of foreign works make their way into English every year.

For a variety of reasons, this particular book seemed to me worthy of translation. A linguistic funambulist above all, Bauçà's radical sense of language is embodied in his abrupt shifts in register, his use of regional/social dialects, neologisms, loanwords, archaisms, the mixing of the learned with the vulgar. His stylistic innovations, his corrosive humor, his fantastic depiction of disturbed minds in claustrophobic worlds, and his refusal to offer his readers an easy ride make him a preeminently original writer.

If every translator faces the problem of how to communicate cultural difference, it is especially difficult to translate from Catalan, for we lack in English a sense of the literary and cultural traditions that have produced Catalan literature, something that does not occur, for example, with French. If English-language readers are generally unfamiliar with Catalan literature, and Bauçà has never been translated into English, how does the translator help to make him intelligible? One way is to translate him into a tradition we *are* familiar with.

Much as did many of his initial critics, I saw Bauçà's writings as being primarily in the line of Samuel Beckett and Franz Kafka, writers who were also experimental, fantastic, intense, and constrained. Bauçà's style and language, his frequent recourse to the ludicrous and the bizarre, the sharp curves of his non sequiturs all struck me as Beckettian.

To aid in interpreting and translating these novels, I developed a lexicon of representative words and phrases from Beckett's novels and at strategic points intercalated them where there was a semantic correspondence with the original. The intertext with Beckett is intended to enable the reader to recognize the familiar, even if the familiar is beyond our rational understanding.

*

What sort of title could encapsulate the three novels in this volume? I suggested *The Siege in the Room* as a nod to Samuel Beckett, who used the phrase to refer to his extremely productive literary period between 1946 and 1950. I intended the title, however, in a more literal sense, as a way of highlighting the constant sense of menace and impending battles, the growing hysteria of Bauçà's narrators. Each of the novels collected here could be interpreted, I believe, as a battle that takes place in the claustrophobic space of the narrators' lives, or within their besieged minds.

Martha Tennent

Barcelona, January 2012

Acknowledgments

This translation benefited greatly from consultations with several people: most especially, Maruxa Relaño, but also Caterina Riba, Carme Sanmartí, Lluís Satorras, and Víctor Martínez-Gil. I am indebted to Jeremy M. Davies, editor at Dalkey Archive, for many helpful suggestions. The introduction profited from consultations and meetings with Jordi Coca, Bauçà's friend and fellow writer, and Amor Estadella, Bauçà's longtime companion; they kindly provided two of the photographs reproduced here. My greatest gratitude goes to the Catalan specialist, Dolors Juanola, who helped me puzzle my way out of many of Bauçà's well-laid linguistic traps.

THE SIEGE
IN THE
ROOM

Carrer Marsala

Maybe the world hasn't always been sad. When we say our words are dragged down by inertia, we mean that what we learn as a pup stays with us. The same applies to other things. Girls, for example, use the phone but don't know its precise function.

I spread my fingers. Carefully I study the outline of their bones. Who can deny me this innocent activity? More than one person might be annoyed by it. Many people believe that it's impossible to agree with all your neighbors at the same time. Faced with this situation, isn't it only fair to choose what best suits me?

Okay, it's obvious: If trees tremble, I tremble as well. Water also trembles when the sun beats down on it intensely for a moment. Water doesn't offer much resistance because it's so strong. The sun too is strong. Truth is, only men mete out blows. Yes, men deal blows, walk upright, and must make a real effort to avoid bumping into each other. (I myself know just how hard it is not to elbow someone.) Women, in contrast, paint their lips. They also walk upright. Red is the most suitable color, despite the dictates of fashion. Observe, therefore, the enormous tension that occurs when an upright man bumps into a woman with painted lips. This mute violence is difficult to evaluate. Herein lies our inadequacy. Perhaps worms, perhaps all the insects that move down below have grasped this, but we'll never be able to ask them. And what about the guy perched on a rock, his fishing line cast out? Wouldn't you say that he also helps to clear the air of tension? I think he does. At the very least, that's what I'd like; we shouldn't exploit our strength. So here we are then: man, woman, and fisherman. We could also throw in a seagull or a pigeon. That would increase the number of variables and remove those responsibilities that overwhelm my natural capacities. This pigeon, this seagull, they can't imagine how good they are for me. They keep me from being such a grouch, they momentarily subdue me. Yes, completely subdue me. If I continue thus, I'm bound to find consolation. And after that, I can launch into other ventures, other transactions. Ones that from the very beginning will bear the stamp of success.

I can't go out today: I'm afraid. I know I have two gold molars, which, incidentally, are well-placed molars. Regardless of whether it's of any interest, I'll mention that these two gold teeth comfort me greatly. Two well-placed gold molars. At first, I felt that the dentist shouldn't have positioned them as he did. But there you are. I don't know if this made me happy or sad—I'm referring to the uncertainty. On the one hand, it strikes me that it would be better to know if a dentist can—or cannot—set molars properly. Not leave matters to sort themselves out. But on the other, we have the lush attractiveness of chance, a premise that does not require confirmation. This leads me to believe that I have always invested too much in my desire to anticipate events, coveting guarantees. For that reason I should instruct myself along these lines: If I do not have a woman by six o'clock, I can always jerk off. Clear, invigorating instruction. Another directive: If the hummock known as Turó de la Fosca didn't exist, then we'd have Turó dels Solcs. Things are becoming more and more simplified. If we don't have one thing, we have something else that is equally pleasurable and will still produce a tickle in our innervated throat. And this tickle is the world axis—as the wise monk used to say.

This wise monk came down from the mountain, through the woods, at eight o'clock every Sunday to celebrate Mass. In truth, he didn't bother anyone. If he ran into the swineherd, he greeted him and continued on his way, down, down, to the village. The veterinarian's wife could have spruced herself up a bit more if she'd wanted to, but she always dressed for Mass in a sensible fashion, in harmony with the customs of the area. She never hurried out. At home, her flowerpots and vases constituted an additional incentive for order: She positioned them on high gothic pedestals. The woman who lived in the house opposite owned a dog, a calm one. It would lie at the door, its tail outside. The vet's wife would leave, the monk would arrive. But none of these events still occur today. They have been supplanted by others that are more difficult to interpret—for example, different methods of waging war.

Have certain combat methods gone out of fashion? From what I understand there used to be several different forms. War existed before. It appears to exist today, but its presence is now veiled. Yes, maybe it's disguised and I don't recognize it. But even if that is the case, on certain mornings I can clearly distinguish trucks full of armed men. No doubt on their way to some front. I've never been able to follow them: I have to catch the bus in the opposite direction—or at least in a different direction. I'll buy the newspaper this afternoon. I'm embarrassed. I shouldn't be. I don't know if I can help it. It's only partially my doing. Many factors beyond my control exonerate me.

I type and I'm afraid of hurting myself. I breathe deeply. I brush my teeth. The hair on the right side sticks up. It doesn't matter. Not a problem. My stomach continues to quiver. I feel no solidarity with my neighbors. Not now. Maybe later. I'm thinking about one in particular who wanted to manage a fleet of taxis, create an empire in a fog-shrouded city in the west; now he's forced to sell walnuts and hazelnuts in a shop by the market. I'm not responsible for his misfortune, but still it distresses me. How will he manage? Will he be able to bear it? Will he know how to handle the housewives' jokes? If the time comes, will he know to stab himself with the fountain pen his uncle left him? No. Because he lost it that afternoon on the jetty. Maybe somebody will find it one day when they cut open the belly of a fish? No, not that either, because today fish know that pens should not be left in the hands of children, and they have stopped swallowing them. May God help him.

I stretch out on the ottoman. I hear the muffled noise from the street. I'm grateful for it, because I know the neighbor in the next apartment has lances standing in one of his rooms. Lots of lances. He's smeared them with first-class oil so they won't rust. He says one day his cohorts will need them. I think my neighbor's a warrior. We don't greet each other much, and when we do, we often switch languages. It´s obvious that neither he nor I wish to identify ourselves. No doubt we have reasons to justify our behavior. We have things to conceal. But even so, he knows that I know he has these lances, and I know that he knows I have nothing. I believe these misunderstandings occur too frequently. As matters now stand, I see no way out. The same thing happens on the days when husbands in the building can't fulfill their conjugal duties in an acceptable fashion. The landings of the stairwell turn into a nest of whispers and nerves. Of course, if a sneaky salesman should unexpectedly appear then and start suggesting we put up brass plates on our doors . . . That, willy-nilly, diverts people's attention and relieves the strain. Even so, it's a fragile equilibrium. The concierge, a driver for the SWAT team, often sends his wife over to annoy the neighbors. Before, I used to think she enjoyed it. Yesterday I could tell it was just a question of conjugal obligation. I understand that the concierge needs to behave in this way: To drive a SWAT vehicle is a nerve-wracking business. Not because these units do anything special, but because of the violent contradiction between his job title and actual duties: To keep supplies balanced they transport eggs from one farm to another and organize a parade once a year. And that's it. In any case, people have lost their taste for clashing with these units. They prefer to devote their time to quotidian concerns.

I too have issues. Yesterday, for example, my beloved wanted to go to a lecture. She invited me because she felt guilty. By the grace of God, I was unable to attend. In the meantime, she comes to me and says I should be grateful to her for inviting me. This means she's cheating on me without knowing why—just feels like it—and on top of that she wants me to suffer through the talk because the lecturer has invited her and she can't refuse. Besides, she wants him to see me accompanying her, have it rattle him. The lecturer isn't exactly her lover, nor is the other bloke with whom she'll cheat on me again tomorrow. Yet, despite all this, she had the mistaken idea that I'd be capable of planting myself on a bench in that conference hall. As I said, I got out of it purely by chance. With this as a starting point, I was able to unravel all the twists in the situation. I finally gave up because I kept getting lost. She, on the other hand, ran down to the street and nervously hailed a taxi. I observed her from the balcony, feeling uneasy for a moment. When it was clear that I wasn't to blame and could do nothing more, my guardian angel gently lowered the blinds and closed my eyes.

That's how I've made it this far, triumphant. And with legs light, I tread on round stones edged by discreet grass. Perhaps the sun is too cruel for the dead who rest on the plain. I could abandon the spiral of sweet violence that wafts from these ashen castles. I could pray, make the sign of the cross, follow the Stations of the Cross. Like flowing water, I could fly madly through the cables and tramlines. It would be better, however, if I sat in distinguished chairs, even if there I'd feel the shudder of emptiness. It's time to produce the linchpin, place it where it belongs. Over and over. If I do this, tomorrow I won't feel like stuffing myself grotesquely with unplucked swallows that I cook whole but can't enjoy.

I write and my fingernails are clean, clean as my aunt's. She lives by the train station, a widow, sterile. She's been to Tangier—who knows, maybe even to Algiers. Of course that was many years ago, when her husband—sterile as well—was in the prime of life and earned a reasonable salary. He left her with no pension, and now she has to scrape by with a bit from every side of the family. The problem is there's nothing attractive about the way she conducts her visits. She arrives, plops herself down in the dining room, nothing lively about her, unable to dissimulate the fact that the only justification for her behavior lies in the cupcakes we leave for her on the sideboard. Yes, she utters a few words to the canary, but that's all. We'd be so grateful for a surprise, a change in character. If she'd just break a bone or vary her interests.

We need, however, to be patient and understand that we are condemned to remain rooted to the ground, or even worse, constrained—like a scapular between our skin and this blue T-shirt. We can't let the star standing at the front of the stage confuse us: The brilliant music performed by a great orchestra emanates from the pit. We must recognize that we will have problems with substitutions or replacements; this happens, for example, when making contact with office girls. It's been pointed out that young women are at their most enticing between seven and nine in the morning, on the trajectory between home and factory. Now that it's summer, the streets beneath the plane trees are damp. Bare-armed girls grasp folders filled with stencils and balance sheets. You encounter more of them on certain buses than on others. The thing to do is to stand very straight, be pleasant, alert, and bold. One method would be to carry a thick folder and amble up to a girl in a blue polo shirt who is seated, reviewing her English lesson, and forthwith let the papers drop onto her exposed thighs, causing her to lean down to pick them up. A more direct attack? It might be more elegant, but extremely dangerous: I'm aware that girls often slap their most intense admirers on buses. City Hall knows this but turns a blind eye. Once again matters are dealt with by means of improvisation and stealth.

It's like when I was working in that office and had to put up with a rather contemptible colleague. For more than a year, with no respite, I had to suffer his abominable comportment. Not even the splendid nights could relieve me of the anxiety for which he alone was responsible. I was consumed by a dull, piercing hatred. Frequently, for example, as I marched up the broad staircase with its crystal knobs, landing after landing, I would encounter him coming down, dragging first one foot, then the other. That's how he managed both to irritate me and entertain the head of personnel who, consequently, came to disparage me in turn. It's true that I tried to find a way to get under my colleague's skin. I would phone him late at night, but he would take the receiver off the hook. I also talked to his lover, the company's telephone operator. Nice girl. A magnificent girl, in fact, who was meant for me. However, as soon as he realized what I was up to, he rushed in. They're married now and have six kids. They say he beats her. Sometimes we run into each other by the port, and right away he offers me potato chips. He doesn't like them, but I must admit he certainly knows how to get the most out of the abrasive sound of cellophane wrappers. I've never figured out how he realized it irritated me. When will the torment end? Probably not until he kicks the bucket. Only then will I find repose. After that, I can confront my own death unafraid, greet it openly, let death get on with it.

But for now: My teeth continue to maltreat my tongue, tar is black, spouses pause in front of shop windows, I could be attacked from one instant to the next, or be treated quite unfairly, as though I were a murderer. The only calming consolation I find is to stare at the gardener who saturates the orchard grass, so pleased with himself. The water runs gently through the Gramineae. He's a public servant, satisfied, happy. I'll spell it out. He always wears a uniform, blue, that he prefers on the large side. Married. Has two daughters who set off for school very clean. Yes, he's a fortunate man who waters the garden. Does it well, without splashing mud on the stems of the plants. Has a degree, but doesn't set much store by it. Says the important thing is skill. That may well be the case, but he had to get a degree, something his father never did, a man who spent his whole life repairing locks on doors, cupboards, and drawers. He too was a satisfied man. The gardener's wife even more. She comes and goes, goes up, comes down, greets the neighboring woman, the concierge, and the vegetable man. She repeats the latest jokes to the woman behind the counter at the butcher's but doesn't know how to remove the splashes of blood from her clothes. Self-assured and haughty, she returns from market laden with promises.

To fortify myself, I could reflect on the engineer who studied at the *Alta Escola d'Estudis Normals*. That's where he learned to design a new kind of reinforced-concrete beam. He has a thorough knowledge of how to turn a profit; many people consult him on that account. This allows his days to elapse in a sensible, exemplary fashion. No coercions, no assaults. His apartment is top-notch, but not ostentatious. He dresses elegantly, moves gracefully. No secret foibles have been detected. Many citizens have taken him as a model for their own lives, which always border on mediocrity.

This architect should represent something for me. It's an acknowledged fact that you can acquire prestige by wearing the same tailored suit as he does. Just as it's also true that if you flagellate yourself at night, you'll experience a degree of gratification. Furthermore, if we can limit ourselves to sewing the button where we need it, with no sign of vanity, we are certain to be blessed. Hence, anything could be possible. For example: I stand stock-still and fix my attention on a *coca de llardons*—that pastry crust filled with pork cracklings. Do I sing? No. Despite the fact that I adore blue-and-white checkered tablecloths, I have to be cautious. I have to be familiar with the route from table to toilet. I need to have it marked out: short walk, firm stride, mouthful of spittle. It all boils down to having a plan. Like everyone else, I require a lot of medicine. I still don't have all I need. This causes me considerable confusion, so I improvise in order to deal with it. The typewriter stops, then starts up, again and again, as if it wanted to go somewhere. If I am patient, don't get frightened, it comes to a halt—no burnt lips, no visits to my cousin. Let the sand let itself be lapped by the water, as is befitting. I realize that I'm climbing the mountain now, on the side where I will escape my enemy. The men pursuing me have stayed below, for the time being. If I don't fall, if I'm not spotted, I'll be able to rest at the top. I hear shouts and cover my ears. I rest beside the clock. Tangier! I should have gone to Tangier in 1920, with a felt hat. It's far away now. Tangier no longer exists. Not that sun, not 1920. The road to resignation is long. Excited heart, burnt tablet. I caress my fingers and fumigate as I grope my way along. And me, don't I excite the neighbors? I frighten myself again. Can I state that I am truly satisfied? Will the professor's daughter love me in an appropriate way?

Amid all this, the rumor circulates that one thousand two hundred and thirty seagulls have been executed on the Isle of Cabrera. They had been transported by ship from Barcelona. There, under great secrecy, they were locked up in police stations. Police stations crammed full of papers.

A black girl—from Guinea or Cameroon—managed to obtain graphic information on the execution. A girl whose hair hummed when the wind blew from the side. She kept a trunk with rabbit skins and the trunk stood by the door, a raffia hat from the previous summer on top. She sang songs of devils and as a rule kept her diary up to date. She spoke of her marriage to a man from Vinebre, but he abandoned her early one morning in the square. She had tasted the waters of many fountains and had filed her nails on many beaches. And a famous writer had kissed her skin while his mother was still alive. When it rained, she would slip up the coast where she kept a dark-skinned young lad, large and love-stricken. A black girl who knows what she wants. She takes the measurements, calculates the number of bricks, and in a snap her little house is built: a cottage in a style we would all recognize as our own. Her hands are warm, yet it's never occurred to her to hurl herself from her bed to the patio to generate conversation amongst the neighbors. With large eyes she sizes up her relatives, who tend to side with her because what she says can always be proven. To a certain extent.

And the rest of the population: What do they think? Where do they live now that it's turned hot? If I approach, I'm sure they'll attack me. I suspect they are preparing for combat. For some time now their grins have grown more pronounced. I, on the other hand, am joyless. I need to really set myself to the task and assemble a nice collection of shirts in muted tones. This must be my mission.

How is it that Lluís manages to dress better every day? The buttonholes on his shirts, for example, more and more match the color of his trousers. No doubt that is why his wife has finally been able to sing at the Opera House. They suffered long years of pain, never daring, always believing it impossible. Now she just sweeps in, quite determined. She knows that nothing sags, her shoes are polished. The concierge greets her with a frank smile. One more sign that things are coming together in an orderly fashion. Cheered by this news, I raise the blinds and put away my pencils. I can stop thinking about the skulls of our deceased citizens. Let them rest, wherever they are. With this in mind, I am able to cast my gaze courageously in any direction, stare down the madmen who terrify me, and approach them. They address me and describe their lives in precise terms. Last night, the sages must have discovered another source of information; the matriarchs will be encouraged to shine their doorknobs with greater enthusiasm.

And me? How can I rise to the occasion? To begin with, I can water the flowers—provided the neighbor doesn't threaten me on the stairs. If he starts organizing tactical maneuvers, I'll be forced to put sandbags at the door. I will, if necessary. Other than that, I could stroll over to the Plaça de Sant Frost and scrutinize the impressive barracks. I could also go down to the street, go out. The stairs aren't properly buttressed. I'll have to be careful I don't break something. Nothing will be broken without my intervention—or perhaps only what should be. I can't imagine what it would be like if something collapsed. Whatever it is, I couldn't possibly deal with the situation now. Better if the staircase just shifts slightly and then settles. Like Cicerone, who laughs at me, hanging up there in the painting. Like Senyor Tomàs, who has studiously disguised himself as a pirate in order to go into the garden and smell the begonias. Like the housewife, who hangs up clothes—the pins in her mouth— while dispensing precise instructions. These facts prove that the enemy has stripped the houses bare. I sense their approach—their mouths foaming with their desire to assault me, punish me in an exemplary manner. Though it's pointless, I can reason that perhaps they'll be exhausted after climbing the steps. But at least one of them will manage to interrogate me: What are my most intimate beliefs, where do I urinate, do I have fresh towels and a disinfectant ready for after the beating? One hope remains: that the few female neighbors who support me will soap down the edges of the steps so the riffraff will stumble and be dashed to pieces.

No reason for me to be afraid. In truth, we should never repeat anything without a valid reason. We can't allow ourselves to be strangled by repetition. Each gesture should be progressive. It was about time, for example, that priests rid themselves of their cassocks. Good Lord, how many years of that black garment! Such a terrible lack of elasticity. And of course they couldn't move around freely, because right away everyone would see they were servants of the altar. Today, in contrast, they can go wherever they please. They're quick and can slip sideways into an elevator when it's a matter of uttering a few words to a lady dying from breast cancer. Soothing words, simple, appropriate. Then, on leaving the ailing woman, they can scurry directly to the Archdeacon's house or else stop by the printers'. In short, all the circumvallating of today's uncassocked priests is worthy of comment, analysis, and attention.

I myself should be taking steps. I could acquire a ground-floor house with an alcove and a bedside table, all of it in the penumbra. A crucifix above the escritoire. Linen sheets, according to my beloved's wishes. I could run my fingers, with such a sense of satisfaction, along my throat and double chin. Wait till I feel sleepy. First consult Ausiàs March, then Jordi—as in Sant Jordi, a.k.a. Saint George. With their permission, feel my way into the forbidden chamber and defile it. I enter. A cat stretching itself on the railing makes my cock stiff straightaway. I have an erection in the semi-darkness. I go no further. Nothing has happened. Rain begins to fall. A child cries. A woman shouts, "*Carles.*" Once again I notice my defenselessness. Pain attacks me. I must prepare for war. Saliva rolls out of the crack in my mouth. I leave. I brush away an insect that has spotted me. When I arrive, I'll play the harmonica to the point of lividity. That's the thing to do.

Rather than indulging in other cruelties, such as killing rabbits at the break of dawn. Even more unpleasant if the hunter wends his way alone, without noisy camaraderie. To grasp these animals by the ears and deliver the final blow on the back of their furry necks is *not*, as the English say, fair play. It's taking advantage of their magnificent ears. If we like the fact that they have long ears, we should find a different way to sacrifice them. Gas them? No, that would leave them stiff; they'd seem human. No one would want to eat them. A blow to the neck is, of course, more graphic, more cruel, more dynamic. Harry them with gunshot? The animals would burst open. In that case, we mustn't stare at the cadavers. Lackeys pick them up and stack them in wicker baskets. The noble hunters who fired the shots and the lackeys who collected the animals do not exchange glances. It all comes to an end when the farmer's wife marks the rabbits' noses with a little cross and cooks them with rice and marjoram. The party concludes when the host's daughter, mounted on a horse and dressed in riding habit, is lifted from the saddle by her admirer.

A theory is going round that the loins of a gentleman's daughter are more delicate than others, and this comforts the baby during pregnancy. It is true that when these women are with child, they walk slowly and in the evenings dream of the eyes their infant will have. They loathe the smell of the chauffeur's shoe polish when he arrives to announce that everything is ready. Everything is ready for the visit to the cousin from Colombia. The Colombian lady wears a pretentious hat with a large blue bow. Her husband is named Mancini, her daughter Anita. This Mancini has a business, he imports vinegar. Even owns a large ship to transport his vinegar, one that sails admirably across the ocean. A vessel painted with two stripes: blue and ochre. His brother-in-law—the name's Odó—has a small airplane and often crosses over the vinegar-bearing ship in mid-voyage. They signal each other from ship to plane. Over in Colombia the indigenous people roll large casks into shipyards that are used as warehouses.

Many people do their work satisfactorily.

Many women know how to hang their stockings correctly. Girls carefully arrange their hair on either side of the part. Priests maintain their soft skin, and an intelligent expression that allows them a glimpse at our sins. Any maneuver to distract them is useless. But then it's not particularly satisfying to go to confession either. We soon realize we have other reasons to worry—liver problems, kidney stones—which will not vanish with a simple, meticulous confession. Beyond that, we still have the architecture of games. For these reasons, one finally accepts defeat and stops confessing, or rather admits to whatever sin, in whatever fashion, as long as it sounds acceptable.

All of this because the country possesses a certain thickness, and strong winds carry away our sand structures, wafting them to dead deserts. We must react, we must always start anew. Only on a few, specific days does the light burst forth, for instance now on the boulevard called the Paral·lel, as I stroll, pure and clean, accompanied by no futile terrors. It is eleven o'clock. The sun shines on my excellently clean teeth. A few pedestrians notice them and lower their eyes, or—according to their character— smile at me. I pay no attention to one or the other. Fearlessly, I trundle along. Not even the huge, wheezing trucks can deter me. They're probably from the town of Flix—or maybe Carcaixent. I proceed. City Hall invites me to telephone. A refulgent phone booth advances toward me, embraces me. I phone. I phone a person who has just washed and placed a drop of seductive perfume on her breasts and ears. She lives on Carrer Calàbria—Calàbria Street. I say nothing. I hear only her soft panting. I hear her hair taking wing in the wind I know so well. The wooden sideboard holds an aquatic plant and an iridescent fish. There is no fish in the case of the neighbor who leaves her apartment to buy flour. The person listening to me covers her thigh. She no longer gazes at the horizon. I hang up without resentment and quickly escape the phone booth. I realize, however, that I will sin again on another sunny morning.

What if I take steps toward veritable repentance? There's still time. That way I could walk with my heels flat, parallel to the edge of the sidewalk, remove my hat without hesitation. Yes. I need to wash my hands and find my way to an address that is clear, to a door with a number, a street with a precise name. There, I will grow fond of translating, of accommodating things to things. And when the time comes, I will perform sensible ablutions, comb my hair, tie my shoes. There, the judges will not fill me with dread, even though they carefully truss their documents, binding them only in onyx. That's why I have to promise myself never again to laugh on the phone. It's not proper, not healthy. This conclusion liberates me. Or at least it allows me to pull my teeth, one by one, or spit them into the kitchen sink, bouncing them against the porcelain. It allows me to visit a distant city where on the train platform I meet a charming, cheerful excursionist wearing a canvas skirt and white socks. A girl who never thinks about the Vice-President, who also dresses in white, wears a blue sash, and fulfills his duties—especially that of entering and leaving his car, which is driven into and out of the garage in a consistently neat manner. In the meantime, all trains escape up the coast, heading toward France. I can't prevent it. My neighbor comes out, then goes back inside to lock up her cat. She sees an injured person on the street. This will make her late to work. She will be punished, lose her job, lose her cat. And I won't be able to prevent it.

I need to be on the alert, pay more attention. Everything becomes fragile if in excess. I must slip my fingers carefully between the bowls and the bottles. Even if I should hear a crash, no sudden somersaults. The town official might find it suspicious and have me returned to the old prison that is still plastered with proclamations from the last war. Perhaps tomorrow we'll be ordered back there, to drive armored trains that don't hesitate before firing on the bell towers of Jaca. Let's hope this time we will have planes and drones and sharp-eyed pilots.

Today, however, is Maundy Thursday. I'll give the railing a coat of rustproof paint, even though the fish must be just like the ones on that island. I know the hail is the same. My fingers are still bent, and I establish a set of values as I read, the way everyone does who reads or researches. Do vices—or bad habits—still hold their former prestige? In any event, I can use words without receiving some terrible punishment. Many devices work. All of them are accessible to a greater or lesser degree. I can apply them the way any user would: fast. Lots of little devices that have their own merit, a certain vitality, a certain consistency. Countless different tastes exist. We should stand plumb, grasp a particular taste, and memorize it so we can reproduce it at the proper hour. Here now is something that satisfies, offers guarantees, and allows you to obliterate your tomorrow and to warm the air. We also need to create an energetic discourse that will aid us in establishing ourselves at the Palace: the Palau de la Generalitat, the seat of government. There's a tremendous muddle there now; the children are keeping close watch over the assistant's accounts. The fellow's only option is to make it with the Mrs. Then we'll announce that the boss has been cuckolded, and this will force the bailiffs to stop by when making their rounds. As a result, a stench sweeps through the dining room, and, naturally, what's been announced bears no resemblance to what's finally served. Life at the Palace is contentious. The blight is spreading, causing sportsmen to scribble their names in foreign languages.

I won't paint the railing.

And furthermore, that viscous woman plays the piano. She says she's recording, going to Paris. Why does she tell these lies? Isn't it enough that she offends me? Doesn't she realize it is not my intention to rape her? I don't deserve this. The problem is my *trousseau* isn't good enough to seduce the other woman—the one from the Nocturnal Adoration Society. This is the first step. I know of others who have succeeded. My grief is great, it's choking me. The old man who is presently lowering the blinds also saddens me. He's standing behind them now, but who knows what coarse act he might have committed. Or will tomorrow. What the ads state is not true, viz. that people with tremendous energy exist and are in possession of such a deep desire to live that they are capable of replacing their bathroom tiles. Presumably they are married, with children, people with might. It has also been asserted that some elderly poets have never stopped writing opuscules. One thing only is clear: The Archbishop has left and this has not altered our precarious situation in the least. Women continue to bathe behind emery-polished glass. Carpenters create the usual sawdust. Mouse tails are the same length as ever. No one expects anything, which is why insurance companies prosper. Rain falls vertically, as always. Suicides leave the same notes, some quite humbly publish them in newspapers. Girls named Lisa don't realize that the color black suits them. Brothers-in-law of every tribe continue to fish on Sundays. Water flows if it encounters a slope. She-asses don't swallow rhubarb on meadows. Flour-dusted cats lick themselves under the stairs. Landowners organize horseraces. Guitar strings need to be touched. Poor folk conjure up shadows that approach Grandmother's forest. Walnuts fit in a clenched fist. Corpses quickly become bloated.

And no doubt the dogs will appear. Surely, fear is justified. The effect of the ointment is beginning to wear off. If I apply more, won't my skin start to peel? Nothing of value can be done without light. All the same, I can set the process of salvation in motion, even if I do hear low-flying bombers. I could stab myself. She'd appreciate that. The dead bodies on the beach can wait. Everyone knows that salt slows putrefaction. The fact is I find myself at present on a plateau. Who could possibly dislodge me from here? I love myself more on this high place, and I wouldn't have to sell blacks in Abyssinia. The solution is love. Volpone or Jacopone? I'll use the latter on the horsewoman next week. She too has been to Ferrara, where I'm sure she strolled about wearing a cape.

She—Diana—stares at me. Will I get a hard on? I could, if I wanted to. Diana, with her blue eyes, perseveres. Maybe I should turn my back. She can make only the most local movements: A slight flutter of her robe stirs the air, sending me the faintest of breezes. No need for me to do anything vulgar. Nothing obliges me. Not even the sensible man who crosses the square, Plaça Gran, every afternoon. That sensible guy is heading to the neighborhood of Sants, because he lives in Sants. But he could strike anywhere. He's dangerous. His mobility is offensive. It would be stupid to underestimate his effectiveness. Even so, he's not ruthless unless you get too near him.

It's over now. Diana has rushed off to check on the stew. It's drizzling. The sensible man crashed his bicycle near the town of Cerdanyola. Diana returns. It's great the way she moves her ass when she goes up to the roof terrace. I've got flat feet. That's why I've removed the lid from two very old boxes. I sniffed them for a moment, put a weight in each pocket, and took a short walk. It was a good idea: Some half-witted girl followed me. I couldn't make out what it was she wanted. When a cat meowed, I turned the corner into the first street. She was wearing a very clean shirt. Had a morning coat in her bag. When I noticed that the cherry trees awaiting me were not lit up in the sunset, I thought it advisable to withdraw. At home, I made a tiny effort to love myself. I didn't succeed. I finally found a comb. Thought it would be the solution. For two hours I sat on the bench waiting beside the chest of drawers. Couldn't make up my mind to comb my hair: I had passed my neighbor on the stairs and noticed a sign of suspicion blazing in her eyes. And with good reason.

I strolled very slowly this afternoon! I think it was because I was following a languid girl. A poet—getting on in years—also followed me for a while, all decked out in his maroon blazer. Told me he'd been to Venezuela. Later, I headed down Carrer Til·lers where Teia signaled me from her balcony. I didn't feel like looking up at her. That's how I managed to reach the end of the street, near the pergola.

I can truthfully state that today I have been kind to everyone.

Tomorrow is Saturday. First off, I've got to make sure the comb's clean. The soap must be dry, not squeaky. The hoist has to function, and then, finally, I will climb elegantly into the tilbury. Will the woman pianist who lives on Carrer Còrsega be there at four? Probably. If she's not sick. On Sunday I'll check out the grape harvesting, or maybe pay a visit to the lascivious hermit. Girls still do not dive naked into swimming pools. Maybe I should go to Buja. Used to be a woman there who had puffy hair and painted her lips. Did she do it for me? In any case, she wanted to. Wonder if I'd see her in Buja. In the meantime I can relax, drowse. When I hear them whistling to me from the garden, I'll decide what to do.

Nothing's forcing me to hurry. Why can't I be cheerful? Nothing's keeping me from it. Everything recommends it. At bottom, it's up to me. All I have to do is refrain from covering my mouth, close my umbrella, walk without being blinded, put away the cornet, unfold the curtains, and light the fire. Businesses should be left to lawyers' children: they know how to play the piano—or at least a polka. They can, if they want to. They have to be coaxed sometimes, especially when a smiling girl steps to the center, brandishing a gardenia. That's a real challenge for them. Then they play. The thought comes to me: We should destroy the leaning Tower of Pisa accompanied by Diana Ross. The trouble is she's often on tour and me in the hospital. The nurses ignore me. It's not enough to faint, you've got to know how to drop the glass without cutting yourself.

Isn't it marvelous to have come this far? Yes. All the more so if I stop to think that should I wish to dance with the goatlike Galatea, I can choose the summer night I believe most apposite. Galatea—always encircled by a starry halo, regardless of whether the moon is shining—is gentle of gesture and form. When she slices the bread, she holds it close to her breast. She makes no crumbs. And if she does, they fall on the tablecloth. Drink brims from the green, bubbled glasses. If she hears the temple bells, she pays no heed, especially if they are marking the eleventh hour. She isn't bothered when the priest jokes about the hairs on her arms; for many years she has ignored hairs and vicars. Now she pays attention only to the fresh fescue growing by the watercourse, or to certain oak trees that stand at the corner of the sown field, to certain pine trees in a grove. In short, she is my guarantee against the disheartenment of touch. Because she is white-hoofed, like her maternal grandfather. How many times have I suddenly awoken in the middle of the night to find her rocking in the chair, guarding the reflections of the moon for me!

I am often told that the sun is obtuse, always the same. Better just to drop the subject. Then it won't be necessary to restore the Elizabethan architecture; that's what one individual I know does every day—an innocent, insecure man. I get in the car and head to the city. The road is bad, and the apricot trees are dying. I leave them behind; only a few remain. My fingers are still thin, but willing to do anything. The sodomite is strolling down the avenue wearing a straw hat. He would never have dared before. Like everyone else he now catches the bus that will take him to the open countryside. Everything is falling into place, of its own accord; now I can put it all behind me. My hands are heavy. The wind is still. That other fellow understands things; he's sure of himself as he strides toward the wharf. As a matter of fact, he treads carefully on the flagstones. He doesn't play games with his Italian sister-in-law. In the meantime, the farmer—one leg in, one leg out—is punishing the grapes that are still green and sour. The sun and wind remain, but even that may come to an end. It all depends on whether the blonde lifts the suitcase or refrains from touching it.

My neighbor raises the blinds in her apartment again. That means they'll be phoning me soon. I won't be able to gaze at the castle any more. I'll probably be impounded. I have to win the lottery. Any of these things could happen. I put on my gloves. I go out. The academic sheltering himself over there isn't carrying an umbrella. Spurred by some interest, he approaches the door to my building and straightaway comes up to me. I can't give him anything. I drop everything and head back to the Paral·lel. Goods are transported up the road. I'm not troubled. All that I have affirmed is true and clear. I have one thing yet to learn: how to properly break up a lump of sugar. Green shutters are green shutters, and for that very reason they are objects of manipulation, attention, and affection. On the other hand, it doesn't matter if night dew is the same as the cold wind known as *celistre*. In a similar vein, some verbal forms are purer than others. And it is at once necessary and possible to distinguish between them.

Women stroll and then sit. They sit down and again handle round balls with fingers pale and clean, thin fingers very different from those of priests. Definitively, it's as I stated: Yarn traverses the sanctuaries. And the beards of rickety old men could use just a touch of the comb—if well executed. One last note. The Falangist, José Antonio Primo de Rivera, is both present and at the margin. Something similar occurred with Franco's *Social Investigation Brigades*. I keep mumbling verses to myself, but I'm not responsible for this. Or for the constant disorder on the train tracks, for that matter.

I could try phoning Grandmother again, but I've decided I'll wait till three o'clock. Is that a long time? It's time that I can devote exclusively to me. I left the dead some while ago, treaded on them. That's why I don't need to shake the dust from my shoes now. Nothing remains of all that. Absolutely nothing. The officials buried them. Let them tremble with rage, like a pack of dogs in a forest grown calm. Let them.

The sun is more and more cold, but very Elizabethan. Now is the time to pluck up our courage. A lot of energy is required if we want to avoid danger and not punish the dog too hastily, which would leave our nerves frayed. So, are there people who live to-gether without touching one other? Maybe, maybe not. In any event, apparently the instinct is to do *something*. City Hall's power resides precisely in the assumption that we live each day and need both to grow stronger and to win victories. That's why the admin-istration permits us to brandish handfuls of hair, even if we admit that we cut it ourselves. With this in mind, aren't we headed for a mad sprint on a chestnut horse, through the heather, toward the summit? My cerebrum is vacuous, depleted by the horsewoman. That shouldn't unsettle me. The crow's flight is also vacuous, but that doesn't mean it's indicative of anything. Not anything I know of. This is not to say that it's impossible for some learned person—maybe that sensible man—to feverishly develop desperate theo-ries amid white lilies. I rush away, racing through a vineyard. It's best to shrink from all contact. I'll have my fill with the carabi-neer's wife who has just moved nearby. That will no doubt cause me considerable distemper. She'll come asking for salt. I'm sure she'll show me her petticoat. I can always entrust myself to Saints Cosmas and Damian. Evil tongues say they were sodomites. That's the rumor they're spreading. These evil tongues lick giltheads and seafood, because to speak of these saints one must live near the sea. Otherwise, it's not convincing. In point of fact, they were maritime saints, even if mariners don't like to recognize this and disdain-fully refuse to name their boats after them—especially if they're trawlers. Though as far as saints go, they are most appropriate.

The brass on the beds in the houses on Carrer Balmes suits the ladies who live there and see that the brass is polished. These gra-cious ladies generally know how to resolve conflicts: They have the Book of Saints constantly at hand. Of course, at times they are besieged by drowsiness. Perhaps this is when they comprehend that their moments of passion are simply a matter of opportunity. They suffer a moment of disquiet when the realization comes to them. But right away the shine on the brass prevails, the child calls out *Mamà*, the husband picks up a pencil and puts on his glasses. Harmony is restored. After a slight sway, tramlines again find their repose. We are allowed to provoke minor disorders so that we can then enjoy the pleasure of the return to quietude. I cannot at this moment, however, take responsibility for these ladies. It's a pity. I wish I could. They often win, and I have to give in, racing to arrange everything: legs, the headboard on the bed, whatever is necessary to avoid committing some intolerable mistake. In effect, my defenses are few. I sometimes suspect that the ladies' shutters are not actually made of wood, though I had assumed they were. My options do not admit verification of this. This distrust, this apprehension will not go unpunished.

I am again sailing on the river, heading upstream. It's not very sunny. The heroic deed is risky. And what was bound to happen, does. The magistrate orders canonshot. It goes off very close to me. The boat, however, is able to continue. The magistrate can't see me now. I seize the moment and go ashore. I burn the ship on the riverbank.

At this point, I must learn to wrap myself in the remaining blankets. Begin by reducing contacts. I'm not a brave sort, but no need to worry. I require special treatment. In order to get started, I have to take precautions—too many—and this automatically implies a decrease in the overall number of transactions. Even so, I know that I will not be spared failures and vilification. For example, she wants to tell me the story of her life. I frighten myself terribly. I know she makes light of it. I leave her sewing. I walk up Carrer Gran. I observe a general who has also lived his life—still does. An awkward girl watches him. The wife isn't present. Perhaps she was one of the women lost in 1940. That erudite man standing over there also seems to have a life of his own. He looks proud, elegant. I greet him as I pass. He shoots me an intelligent glance of complicity. I am aware that events other than these occur in this world. Somewhere a Chinese man hides one slip of paper and takes out another: A radio announcer immediately broadcasts the news to see what the results are. In the Pacific, God extends his antennas and rearranges his bowels. An amanuensis traveling on the Paris-Bordeaux express spreads out his jacket. The fog unravels on the Collserola Mountains. The corporal salutes the lieutenant. The king stretches out on the sofa, the queen on the chaise longue. The mother-in-law who arrived by plane brings fresh cheese. When the child hears the doorbell, he bursts into tears and breaks the vase. *Monsieur Guedaffi* makes his way to the water, pokes a plastic bag with his cane, and returns to the desert. In the end, we all wish that things were sad, but then we must hurry to cover our mouths. Even so, we recognize that this is the only solution. If you stop to think about it, it's only logical that they refuse to give us gun permits.

As for me, I only want to bite her mouth, her tongue. One of those places. But . . . how will I manage? I'll quickly wear myself out. I have no ready strategy at the moment. It's true that I have faith in certain principles, I study certain prestigious models, I deceive myself like all diplomats. And the war hasn't even erupted yet. But I've noticed troops being moved, received cryptic phone calls. Last night I decided I would declare myself unfit. I wouldn't be a valuable player in a crucial battle. My blood doesn't circulate with the necessary fluidity, and a good combatant is forced to experience explosions at close quarters and has to march in the snow. Anyone would fight better than me, throw grenades more efficiently, handle mortars with greater skill. I sense it's not easy for me to accept these thoughts, but I have devoted years to meditation and melancholy. I will, therefore, practice detachment rather than put up a fierce defense in the battle that awaits me. I will fall into the moat unarmed. Yes, I will be knocked down.

Let's put it this way. Somehow, the landing has been gentle. Yes. It's always been that way with my Montgolfier balloon: It rises above Avinguda Pearson and comes to a soft landing by the chimneys in the Besòs neighborhood. The crowd erupts into loud shouts of excitement. The girl on Carrer Topazi appears on the roof terrace. Mature women sigh. It's twelve o'clock. Some men are inspecting locks. Others are planning to see the play by Molière. The season has been launched. By mid-November it will be time for *Hernani*. At this precise moment, I take the occasion to demonstrate my heroic deed. At a time when young girls are endeavoring to have their music boxes restored, children are neither entering nor leaving school, and the great folk-song competitions have not yet begun. Only the farmers are distressed. They wish they could devise a similar attraction, but the municipal government refuses to free up subsidies. City Hall is not afraid of the chaos this might provoke.

As for me, I tell myself that never having visited the town of Sitges beats all records for neatness. Herein lies my honor. Sustained and fortified by this honor, I can elegantly offer the neighbor my hand. As a matter of fact, I'd be quite capable of offering it to her right now. More and more I am behaving according to the laws of Argimon. I wonder where he is. But of course, he must be crossing the bridge in Molins de Rei, on the way to his piano class. In any case, he's no virtuoso. It's true he plays the piano, but he's not good enough to make the paintings on the wall tremble. Pretentious paintings, like everything else about him. Perhaps I'll strangle him when he's returning from class one day. I'll wait for him under the stairs and wind my batiste scarf around his neck till his tongue protrudes. I'm sure he'll let me. That would suit him and the town of Molins de Rei. Only logical. He knows it has to end this way. His wife, in contrast, is much more vulgar: She's never appreciated batiste, never paid me any attention. Who *does* she pay attention to? How can Argimon bear such a degraded state of affairs? There's no hope. He'll continue to play the piano in Molins de Rei, and he won't be struck dead beneath an oak tree. I'll have to strangle him.

Other crepuscular men, however (such as Colombàs, Petrus, and Alcorissa) must still be spitting their way around Malta. I have to leave them now, got to make the wedding cake, sixty guests, come specially from Lourdes. They have no ancestry, no lineage; they'll eat everything. Besides, they always quarrel amongst themselves and spoil the event. What an evening! Summer is lasting too long. I can stand it, for the time being. I'm controlling the moves, setting the traps, like that lass from the county of Conflent, a great cocksucker. Said she wanted to make good use of her time, scurrying from town to town, from Prada to Elna, Elna to Vilafranca. A job well done, wholehearted vocation. Conflent! I might return there one day, but differently, brandishing a flag perhaps, from atop a tank, or sweeping up the sawdust in the foyer of Aunt Lluciana's house. She'll enter wearing a shawl, and I'll lay down the broom and assault her: "Auntie, off with your clothes. Right now." The sweet woman will impishly lick her lips, as she strokes the ribbon on her dress and throws her neckerchief in my face.

But right now someone masquerading as Pharaoh has climbed up to the garret. When he dies, they'll discover the tools in the dresser. People are aware of these incidents. The kid who works at Roca knows it. The canon who walks down the steps—no pallium, no formalities, relieved of all external signs—he knows it as well. It's harder, however, for me to grasp, because I easily confuse cemeteries, even those that are clearly distant from each other—such as Sant Andreu and Santa Coloma. Sometimes I also forget and leave my sister-in-law's lemon dress in the wardrobe. Nevertheless, when I pass the security guards at one o'clock every day, I know to buy the newspaper, smooth my tie, and dust off the dirt that's settled on my muscles. I also save my lovers' blonde hairs. I keep a handful from each of them in separate little boxes in the sideboard.

My arm aches, but everything seems to encourage me to be kind. The new druggist didn't raise an eyebrow; efficiently and serenely he sold me five kilos of plaster. And the bank teller? As soon as he glimpsed me, he couldn't bear for me to stand in line but immediately called out to me, had me pass him the money over the glass window. He never jots anything down when I'm present. Above all, he wants our relationship to continue unperturbed. The lottery-ticket seller? Soon as she spots me, she calls me by name. She's proud that I frequent her business. The man who sells garlic? Puts them right into my bag. In short, I cannot respond to all of these gestures other than by proposing to be more and more good.

Is it necessary to state that we are now like the surging sea? No. But I do need to be on the alert so as not to hurt myself; I mean, not to cut something. I often handle all manner of acuminate, razor-sharp, grinding articles. Moreover, at any moment the barrel of fuel I use for various types of combustion could burst and catch fire. If I'm injured, if something should happen to me, the inhabitants of Ferrara will, of course, continue to make cheese. This thought cannot dispel the memory of the crudeness I have had to endure, and which I'm pleased to have surrendered myself to. I am cheered. But who knows how long it will take to set things right. I'm sure in many ways I'll behave like any one of those thinkers of ours. So, how long will it take me to get cleaned up? No one knows. It's true that I threw myself into this condition. Willingly, happily. No feelings of remorse. But I can feel the dirt affixed to my body, though I avoid looking at it. I don't plan to describe it. I will only mention the motorway and the women who stroll along it. Trees, mountains, rivers, peaches and peach trees (some full, others bare). On the other hand, it's been helpful to learn to cover my ears: The thunder sounds fainter. Also, I no longer have the urge to stab myself in the stomach with the scissors. I haven't seduced anyone. Only a man named Sebastià smiled at me in the final moments, when things were being cleared out, people ready with their bundles. Was that wicked? Was it clumsy of me to have brought out the fan? An inappropriate moment? The wrong color? In any case, it's just another sly story, neither alive nor buried. Only a succession of breaking waves could redeem it from this terribly perverse state. We must keep faith. Ardently, carefully. Let the horns and border passes do the rest. Shall I tell my neighbor about this? I shouldn't, not under any circumstances, but I can't help committing another sin. A sticky matter. I am perfectly aware of the consequences. I have only the consolation of being able to moan close to, and in sight of, my mattress. The same thing will happen again: The woman next door will tell Agnès, and that's how my exercises with her will end. If I let myself become even filthier, this will justify the retreat and prevent other equally onerous attempts. It would be much more felicitous if everything would just settle down and be settled; because in the end, I'll also have to tell Ioia about this escapade. Ioia will want to know the whole story. It's not possible to divide myself between the two of them. Even so, I'll give it a try. They'll spit on me, mistreat me. Me with my air of a morose civet, my saunter like a disconsolate reptile.

I've come this far. Now I can wait for them to come and get me, but I won't be able to avoid seeing them hold their noses. I can't blame them. How many times have I held my own nose! To ask for help would be suicide. Can't take that road, got to find my way out of this as best I can. It's hot. I feel better. Clear sky, clean stars, hard rockets. The trash stays outside. Pianists hurry everywhere. Maybe they love me. It's my fault for not asking them. What if it were a calm love, no attacks, no knife throwing, no thought of going to

Switzerland. But to be loved as one should, one has to have had a blonde mother. Or, at least officially a blonde. Surely it's a well-known fact that we are subjected to constant betrayal. Right now, for example, I live outside the law. I defecated over there, beneath some peach trees that weren't marked with paint. That man I mentioned—maybe he loved me. It must have been because I resembled Aristotle and had stayed at the Waldorf Astoria, or maybe because I like Bordeaux wine. Will he look for me, feel the void caused by my absence? Will there be a burst of frenzy? A free-for-all to determine who will be the first to find me and shower me with gifts? Maybe he'll behave like that girl—the virgin who romped through the thyme, showing her legs, occasionally lending them to us.

I can leave all that. Tamarisks grow there, confident and forthright. Further along lie the towns of Montcada i Reixac and Mas Rampinyo. I won't continue. Today is Monday, tomorrow Tuesday. On the whole, temperatures will fluctuate as usual, according to the season. Will General Spínola issue an urgent order? But, no. I will not make the mistake of showing an interest in this warrior, and I wouldn't consider going to Portugal. I can devote my time to the clocks that betray me because I haven't taken care of them. I know that I still have hope and resilience. Solvency is a different matter. I know how to clean brass—and brass lettering even more so. The Crucified, in contrast, *is* omnipotent. He has turned his back on me. I do the same. All the saints do. You can hear the thick humming of moving hair. The Virgin's voice grows hoarse. This is when it occurs to some pious, spurious man to really go for the dough. The trouble is up there someone coughs in a clear sign of disapproval. Some saintly women release ovules that travel through fallopian tubes to the uterus. Saints who—thanks to the adiposity of certain regions—round out their slenderness in a most charming way . . . Here I could mention that acquaintance of mine: the man with two hearts and three testicles. Better not to. It offends me.

I have a facility for forgetting. Since I don't have to move, I fall and then get up. I don't think less of myself. Not at all. I have lands to leave to my nieces and nephews. I also have nieces and nephews. Why should I have to renounce the idea of offspring? What's the point of abandoning that possibility? Yes, I have some houses, a wife. I am sterile and have nieces and nephews. A vacant lot. A little house with a pergola by the sea, and ten nieces and nephews to dispute it. I'm not ostentatious about my properties, but they know perfectly well what I have. This guarantees that I'll receive visits when I'm in the hospital, on my Saint's Day. Days like that. What more could I ask for? Providence has dictated that it be thus. I was poor, but possessed a rare, sylvan beauty, enough to make Magdalena fall in love with me. She's well-off, relatively wealthy. That's the whole of it. The problem is her embraces are brackish and violent. I don't know where she got the idea they should be like that. But I never wanted to set her straight. Don't know how I could find a substitute for them. We'd get caught up in the game of signing away responsibilities; that always ends badly. Perhaps this sensible ignorance recognizes that things can be repeated, that there can be one-hundred-year-old nieces and nephews, lingering bedroom perfumes, and stores with remnants of varying sizes.

The same thing causes that gentleman to stroll with his tunic gathered about him, feebly glancing around, paying inopportune visits. Of course, such is one's nature. He is learning, but rather too quickly. He's saved by the fact that he knows how to wash his clothes. It's charming the way he twists them. Hangs them up so elegantly. All the women in the building envy him, and he knows it. One has even stopped greeting him. It's worth noting that all the furbelows are stamped with a bunch of arrows facing each other. He distracts the priest during Mass every Sunday. You need a lot of energy to perform all these activities well. I can't do it. I've only just now learned to go to the photographer once a month! I can't compete. This refusal to persevere will not go unpunished.

A great silence has arisen. You can hear the first bombs. They fall on a nearby field. A pigeon flies by. This means the rain will commence at any moment. I try to lie low. I read the newspaper, shame blazes across my face. "Cicero, I command you to appear." He appears. I cheer up. I laugh. With a checkered handkerchief I wipe the ancient, dusty snot from his nose. Compact dust. He smiles at me. "Leave, get out of here." He slips away. Ulysses? You're right, I don't know him.

Everything collapses, the centaurs gallop past. I can't find the bleach or the clothespins. The virgin next door went out to water the cactus; now she's putting the painting back in place. She hangs up the sheets, beats the mattress, puts away the skeins. She reminds me of the girls from Perpignan who were so quick to fall in love. Just encountering a fellow in a maroon blazer could be decisive for them. We know the rest: first comes the house, then the farm, tractor, trailer, and peach grove. Sunday dinner with the cousins who live in Toulouges. Dinner that's mainly green— the fishmonger likes it that way too. Yes, the girls fall in love more easily in Perpignan. That's not a reproach. This way everything is slippery, more welcoming—like the burnished legs of a blackbird. These smiling, timeless girls have never played pétanque. They leave that to their crude uncles who get drunk for no reason, or dress up as Knights Templar to terrify people in houses far from the center of town. Girls from Perpignan always have clean fingernails, and nowhere else in the world can you encounter girls with such consistent, uniform enamel. Of course, not everything is charming. A secret part of their body soon dries up. A fact not often divulged.

My colleagues have been brutally lecturing me about many things these days. Subtle lessons that will produce results later on. Which? Not clear at the moment. I can state, however, that they love me. They are rivals. Vacation time has arrived. Some are leaving town with their wives and a male friend. Others still don't know. They often discuss the women who hover around the cab doors of their trucks. Is that passion spouting from their lips? Not true passion, because the conversation quickly falls away. Nonetheless, they do have to be faithful to the few remaining guidelines. Like them, I should join the Consortium of White Wood. That'd be right up my alley. I'm subtle enough, familiar with wood. Nerves and wood pulp hold no secrets for me. But no, I'll have to give up the idea. For example, I was flogged on the metro today. From among the masses of ugly girls and fat mothers, a spy appeared and struck me repeatedly on the cheek with a pizzle. In view of that, and my cowardly behavior, I've decided not to budge from my rocking chair. I'll reorganize my life, commence a new one. I'm beginning to feel the change; I can tell by the slight cramp in my knuckles. I'll have to protect myself better, determine the thickness of these walls, repair the spot where I place my feet and hands so I won't fall face down. Only then will the horses gallop madly—manes undulating—and not miss the shortcut.

I have to bear this in mind, because Ioia came to see me. Out of the blue she said she wanted to end it all near a reservoir in the province of Huesca. The idea struck me as acceptable—as far as the details were concerned. I'm ready to leave, soon as she wants to. For now, I'll brush my teeth again. It's always beautiful when teeth shine in the grass. I know that Time devours me. It's all a big conspiracy to trap me. I have few defenses. I can only run. That's what I'll do. As a matter of fact, I also have the moons under control. In all probability I will survive the month. I might even make it to the summit, triumphant. I'll encounter wolves, serpents, genets. I'll slip and fall. The moss will be smooth; the viridian green of the rocks will not be intense. After my triumphant climb, I will not laugh. I could, I see that I could. I don't find it necessary. Will that be sad? Trains too are sad (but people board them). As are second sons, sodomites, riverside servants. All of them are sad, but they are used nonetheless; they have their own corners where they aren't pestered by idle housewives.

I put aside these thoughts. I ingest some apricot marmalade, just a tiny bit. It's because I sleep too much, too close to the neighbors. Not enough meters between us, which makes it easy for them to attack me when it suits them. But they won't tonight. They're already asleep. It'll probably happen tomorrow. Tomorrow, I will be completely at their mercy again. Be a good idea to have my bowels ready. I notice I'm starting to love myself. Just a little. Tumbler, plate, spoon: I've managed for all of them to be made of glass or china, alternating harmoniously. The trouble is I'm in a hurry, and the saints aren't big on ambivalence. They tend to tell you either to go in or come out—or, otherwise, to catch the mountain train. Actually, everybody is riding a well-groomed steed. I have the impression they don't even trust the mayor. So why would they pay any attention to me?

Not even General Spínola is successful. So they remove him by force. I could phone him. I won't. I've managed to overcome this very seductive temptation. I'll hold out a little longer. Then I will emerge with renewed ferociousness. People too have their bad habits. I won't be the only one accused. You can bet they also have theirs. For example, today Ioia showed me the strap that tightens her bra—she pulled up her sweater. That is clearly a bad habit. And if she'd been able to, she would have dragged me to Sitges for no good reason, just that bad habit of hers. So, before I sit with the accused, I must bear in mind the manifest incontinence of those who approach me. That's what I have to do, and quick.

I've been pissing yellow for days. I don't think it's anything serious. Sometimes the moon also turns yellow, and it's never anything to get excited about. Despite the sky and the news about the stars. What can be salvaged from all this? A quince perhaps, a couple of orange trees, a jujube. And that's it. Yes, right now I prefer the glass and china plates that I succeeded in putting away.

Everything is drawing to an end. And it's only been two days. My colleagues are starting to reject each other. They're falling apart. Dislocated. They no longer form those lovely ranks with which they won so many battles. They were brave then. They followed orders. Nothing of that remains. No aura. Just a bunch of beaten-down mechanisms. That fellow—succubus—came over just to tell me that he was fucking someone at noon yesterday. What did he expect me to say? Of course, not everyone is a sad sort like him. There's one guy who was on the point of poking a nun—or so he says. He lost his nerve. He did, however, grope her up and down. A white nun no doubt. He must have fallen into the bed somewhere near Terrassa; he often goes there to amuse himself. Despite everything, I am the victim of a terrible deception. Among other falsehoods, the stairs are not actually made of wood. That's why maidservants with their far-fetched plans dine alone. There's nothing appropriate that I can do here, now. It wouldn't help to grow a moustache or stop buying metro tickets. There was a time when these combatants were still wise. They loaded hay onto wagons—wagons pulled by full-uddered cows. Now they're delirious. They say they were born all over the place, have slept with all the women, are experts in all the common vices and virtues. If they haven't been in a prison, they're familiar with a hospital. They have also, as I noted, groped nuns—in front of the bishop or behind his back. Poor bishop! A trembling bishop who travels around on his bicycle and waves his handkerchief to parishioners and the honest lambs who wake early to raise the metal grilles on their shops. I mentioned bishops, but the fact is they haven't been seen for a while now. Some must still be around, however, for a pastoral turns up in my mailbox from time to time encouraging me to follow the straight and narrow path.

Shall I speak clearly? Yes. I have to explain what's going on. I have to proceed with the accusations and charges: no feebleness, no taking sides. Me least of all. This is the only path. The boatswains and cooks on the Transmediterrània ships are waiting; they have placed all their trust in us. They have been very patient until now. The noble thing would be to inform them of the situation, clearly, and not have them wait any longer. Definitively, they should distrust us and try to get out of this, salvage what they can. Let's just drop the matter.

Nobody is on the premises. The windows let in just a bit of light. The chairs aren't aligned. Louis Armstrong is singing "Ramona" behind a satin curtain that billows in the breeze blowing through the slats of the partially lowered blinds. I sit down and stretch my legs. The milkman has the keys and comes in to make a phone call. He's wearing a blue bib and a black tie: He's in mourning for his wife. A boy parks his bicycle against a nearby streetlamp. I'm homesick, I'm nostalging. I have to go home today to play the lottery. The toilet on the train will have run out of paper. I'll have to improvise. Fortunately, I will not be judged, nor—in a similar vein—will I emit judgments about things of which I am ignorant. For example, what do I really know about Portugal? I know the name: Portugal. I know the name of the president—but not the full name. They sing fados, but I'm not familiar with any. It would be onerous to have to tolerate some expert examiner's smile. I should know more because one of my ancestors was Portuguese. Named Rogério. Grandmother never knew anything more than that. The information was transmitted orally. Altogether rather weak. Lacking in density. My name is also Rogério—the matronymic cognomen—but when I walk along a street in a city, any city, pass any of the hotels called Ritz, who would know that my name is Rogério? There is really no value at all in being called Rogério.

I need to do something. Have the tartar removed from my teeth, for example. It's hard to eliminate the muck, but in the end it's rewarding—if it's done with a good dentifrice. The implication is that everything is difficult, but if you keep at it, eventually you get results. Of course it's tiring to rub too long. Then comes the bitterness of defeat. All because you couldn't hang in there for ten minutes—though three would be sufficient if you rubbed energetically. Less and less tartar. The expectation of enjoying whiter teeth increases with each bit of tartar you remove. So white that the lady perfumers will be aglow with love. I know for a fact that I will open my mouth for these perfumers. What sparkling teeth, they will think, what a perfect fellow.

The point is we should be neither wicked nor ambitious to excess. Consequently, I divide up my day into simple actions. I avoid all major risks. Of course a plane could always drop a bomb, or some venomous young guy could blow up the building he's in. This is not altogether impossible; nevertheless, I reject the idea as improbable. On the other hand, the mayor has stated that he doesn't want anyone else to be cremated. It's too hot. For two days now twenty thousand small investors have blocked the entrance to Carrer Gran. Here at home the water is cool; that's why I stare at myself in the mirror. I could always walk over and let the chestnut mare out, put on her halter, pat her smooth cheek, set her free. Let her trot around in the pasture. In the meantime, the bishop has fallen asleep holding the seal in his hand. I advance furiously toward the quarry, where I lie down. I too fall asleep. For a moment I thought I could see Virgil—the street—and the neighborhood of La Guineueta.

I should move to another place. Austria perhaps. Austrian maidens have that blonde fuzz on their buttocks that's attracted the attention of many invaders. Kings still keep scepters in traditional mother-of-pearl cases; cattle still have owners and continue to be self-propelled. Leaves fall as they should. The music issuing from the Ritz is appropriate. People are dancing inside. The Senyoreta wiggles her leg and launches into a step. The leaf falls. The rain falls. One has to accept both falls, as well as the lady's lunge onto the dance floor.

I pass by and proceed onward. I should phone the perfumer. She was disagreeable. She's probably experimenting now with tinctures and scents on the back of her pale hand. I'll leave it for later.

I should run bare-assed to the caves that suppurate gases through the gutters. Can't make the brotherhood look bad: this violence must be at once extreme and circumspect. As I mentioned, it's time for my incursion on horseback. All speculations are invalid. Guards are resolutely making their way up the Rambla. I won't be able to buy the pastry.

I know for a fact that I will catch that bird. Right now I have to be certain that I'm not left with only a handful of feathers. That would be sad. However, if pine needles are sharp, there is nothing we can do about it! Also, the tanks down below are maneuvering on the outskirts of town, and everybody is pleased with the positions from which the basilisks and bombards will sting all who approach. Many seemingly innocent mechanisms challenge me, emphasizing my insignificance. So what if I burst out laughing? That won't fix anything. Insignificant in countless matters. I'm incapable of getting myself as far as Istanbul. I know perfectly well that I will never lay eyes on the Bosporus. Nevertheless, I can't complain.

I can't complain because I was able to know Uncle Genari while he was still alive. He had a sordid philosophy concerning unsatisfactory excursions. He too succumbed. This indicates that refined thoughts in no way prevent a dismal demise. Like the seasons, like insects, death is inexorable. Uncle Genari always carried with him the photograph of a legionnaire. A legionnaire who walked like one. With his neatly trimmed beard, he must have been a cultured legionnaire who had been to Avignon. A tiny medal shone against his chest. No one in the family ever knew the whole story. It's lost in the fog now.

I relocated myself to another spot, to a more advantageous situation, with more incentives. The fig trees swayed parsimoniously. Beneath the white sheet, my hand rested on the maiden's buttocks. Then silently, surreptitiously, she placed her translucent fingers on my crotch. It is possible that Arcadia existed. A tiny angel confirmed it. Considering that things have occurred as they have, it must all be true. Great is this truth. I admit that from this point on, it will be impossible to turn back. I'm plummeting down the slide. Will they come to lynch me today? No need for me to worry. I had better start preparing for war. If not, the same thing will happen again: Weapons will get mixed up (old with the new); there will be a shortage of specialists; on the spur of the moment we'll have to import strategists who won't know the local language or the precise stature of the relief force. Everything done posthaste. That's why wars traditionally last longer here than in other places. The roughness of the terrain is no excuse; it is, nonetheless, a powerful incentive to commence hostilities. Let God's will be done.

As for me, why not marry a slender woman and spend Sundays strolling in the country? I mean, along the barren coast, the scrubland and sea. Never wandering into the brush so the thicket wouldn't ruin her stockings. When we encountered a puddle, we'd jump over it. We would come home in the evening. We would live beside the Plaça de Toros.

Right now, however, I wouldn't be able to tolerate the screeching of harquebuses. Herein lies my weakness. And yet, didn't I suffer the stiff, bayonet-pointed pine needles? Did I not spend an entire month roaming the Montseny Mountains, eating bread and dry sausage? Did I not take part in the heavy-artillery assault on the port? Have I not crushed beetles, made my own dynamite, ruined a lot of tinder? Have I not burnt my fingers more than once?

The columns of smoke that billowed from the battlefield are now extinguished. If my fingers are still rough tomorrow, I won't be able to go to the Estació de França train station. What will he think when I touch him? What solution is there? There's no substitute for a handshake. Can I avoid it by rushing toward the suitcases? Can't let him notice my hands. The look that tonsured man would shoot me! I can't imagine a worse way to begin.

It doesn't matter. The important thing is not to lose my natural, innate ability to disappear. My capacity to enter and exit train stations. The tactful way I speak to the cloistered nun through the revolving *turn* in the parlor of an Ursuline convent. If these trump cards don't wear me down, everything can be saved. I'll be able to confront future storms, perhaps even a potential broken bone.

To wind this up, I experience an apotheosis. After which the waters flow soft, and the barren chestnut trees hazard a reflection.

I wouldn't bathe in it. Not now. Sitting on the riverbank, on the grass that sprouts from the soft earth, I listen thoughtfully to the nightingale. The trees don't distract me. Nymph Aeolia, eager and with perfect cadence, will appear now that I—seated between the water and the horizon—have learned to avoid even the vaguest of passions. I will gaze at her in silence. The invisible pianist and female contralto will sing agrarian songs in the cave. This sense of peace will, nevertheless, come to an end. But in the meantime, I can submit to the austere calm of the chestnut trees. Of course, I have no female tongue handy. The damask is not always ample, hanging loosely; the curtains do not always close smoothly, sealing off the stage. Strange that I've sat here so long and the goldfinches haven't appeared with their screeches of terror and thunderous racket. However that may be, all of us must do what we can, laugh at our own affairs, enjoy our leisure hours—we have to accept the fact that even the inhabitants of Santa Coloma have different customs than the people from Sant Genís. For example. Besides, Ioia lowers the rope into the well better than I do. Should this offend me? I don't think so. In my godmother's tiny garden—over in that direction—blue lilies grow vertically beside the locksmith's. To reach this point, I've had to invest a certain amount of money; the sum involved was small, but now I have the results and know how much more I need to advance. Are the figures correct? I think so. This accounting is exhausting, but it needs to be kept up to date. If it isn't, I immediately encounter dogs on the bends in the road or lying under the stairs. That bit about the dogs is a question of rhythm; by that I mean the manner in which they move their legs. These animals understand fear and terror. But I need not be alarmed by this remote possibility. Better that I observe the ivy, how it climbs the rocks. And it's only ivy. Doesn't the chestnut mare's rump move more elegantly when she captures the scent of sap oozing from generous peach trees gilded by the dawning sun? And cherry trees—with or without sap—don't they blush more gracefully, more genteelly at that hour? My arm hurts, and not even in Sitges are the plotters able to sustain their long-awaited plan. They merely toss about unconvincing words. At four o'clock in the morning, the disgruntled men return to town and place their umbrellas in the stand. I can't follow them. Especially not right now, as I scrutinize the chestnut trees and the soft water, waiting for the passing nymph. Now that I can let go, enjoy the occasional breeze and drowse beneath the confident light of dusk, while the Egyptians calm me by announcing that they have all of eternity to recover the Sinai Peninsula. They aren't in a hurry. They will tolerate the occasional attack; it is only of relative importance. So, no need for me to be concerned about these combatants. I can return to my own affairs, begin arrangements for an agreeable death. Ioia will help me. She knows how to, she's done it before. From now on, I'm placing myself completely in her hands. She has good taste, wears sky-blue, silky chiffons. How different from the turbid day I'm embarking on. It's sure to be filled with malicious incidents. I'll be mistreated by the madwoman in the building who will scar my face with her fingernails. I'll have to apply all my defense mechanisms. Even so, as I've pointed out, I won't be able to avoid a number of minor insults and affronts. Will I allow myself to be brought down? Probably not. What else could I do? Abandon the territory, hastily remove myself to some other place?

I could also stand my ground and eagerly await the siege. This last option would be the sensible thing to do. That is the path to take. Great is my frailty. I will only grow stronger, be revitalized, if I can meet a pianist without husband or children, a woman who's managed to avoid being overexcited by some concert and driven mad. It will prove difficult. Stated more clearly: It's impossible. If this is indeed the case, then I will have rid myself of yet another conflict; I could stroll calmly among the housewives from the better neighborhoods, ladies who dress well, care for their children tenderly, and have unabashed relationships with their lovers. Lovers with simple tastes who learned the elementary rules of their present occupation at an early age.

For no particular reason, things just do not work out well for me. Maybe I should reinforce my various flanks and simply consolidate my situation. I'm willing. The idea is to be certain of the first step and refrain from thinking about the next—even though the first is meaningless if we don't at least anticipate the second. In short, it is necessary to reduce the total number of operations.

I'm waiting.

I'm tired. No mishap has occurred. Should this be attributed to my state of renewed vigil? I doubt it. Again I experience the yearning for adventure. I put on my shoes and go downstairs. Is there any reason for me to feel proud? Yes. Tomorrow will be another day, and the sun will blaze magnificent. The horsewoman will not be the same, nor will Ioia or the madwoman who claws me. I will go out, athletic and triumphant, to buy the paper. Things will be as I envision them; not everything will be the same. If this is not the case, I can always wave my arms around as if I were swimming. What if the horsewoman doesn't come? A shudder courses through my body and I turn green. The ships ignore me. Fearlessly, they continue on their way. I cannot walk on water, and the Good Jesus is grimacing at me. He appears to me first on one hill, then on another. The ships are out of sight now. Lola, who had a breast removed, enters the church of Santa Maria to pray. I can't bear this any longer. I was supposed to sell soap this afternoon. I won't be able to make a single sale. I lost the catalogue. I won't win the prize for best salesman of the season. My cousin has just arrived from Montpellier, and I'll have to invite him to dinner. My other cousin—a girl—refuses to sew the buttons on my shirt. I can't go to the barbershop like this. The relative who's coming laughs too loud, and all my neighbors are removing knives from their drawers and conspiring on the landings. And here I am, unable to enter Paradise. The false prophets that were announced have now arrived. They look like kindly folk, but underneath they promulgate perverse doctrines. I've stained my little cotton shoes; they were my last hope. If it's true that none of you will come to my aid, then for heaven's sake just tell me so, and I'll find something else. If I have to change my line of work, I'll be forced to visit the Ateneu, my literary society.

The horsewoman is not coming.

Obviously, I'm jealous. There's nothing I can do about it. If I were a pilot, I'd fly up and paint some charming fantasy in the sky. She would immediately dismiss her lover and open the window. However, I am not a pilot. Nor am I Mercè Rodoreda or Mercè Managuerra, and I can't hunt rabbits in the scrubland. The greyhounds would never believe me in this condition.

The horsewoman does not appear.

If I had given her that blue silk dress with the black satin trim, maybe I wouldn't find myself in such a dead-end, asphyxiating situation. I need to calm down. Examine the tools: the blades, the handles, all the little mechanisms in between. In short, review everything I need in order to keep the geraniums slender. Everything necessary to obviate that crudeness of thought so prevalent in salaried drivers—and others who assess our network of roads. I have to wrap the twigs carefully so no one will hurt them or knock them onto the street. This is an enormous, disagreeable undertaking. I might have to be present at this ultimate defeat when I witness tires stripping the fibers from the stems. I must remain calm. Avoid only the most unsettling mishaps. As to the rest, let God speak. Let Him do what He can. The choirs of the Adventist Churches could also lend a hand. The departure of the sailboats en masse could prove quite inopportune. And if I don't restrain myself, the world could cease to be round, a fact that would place the crowns of kings in a very uncomfortable state of affairs, and would necessitate correcting children's schoolbooks. More and more I am assailed by the fear of these dangers. Unless I can immediately establish myself in a hotel in Utah, I'll start to tremble and smash my dishes. It will begin to rain. A nervous, absurd rain. I attempt to open and close the windows. Quite pointless.

The horsewoman won't let me go about it with the elegance it requires. Maybe all this moving from one place to another has dulled me. When I swallow saliva, I no longer know what it tastes of. It's my fault that the ladies have become somnambulists. The priests I used to bump into have left now, or only perform in private. But probably not much can be done about it. The shade of the linden tree is not always the most propitious. Moreover, on certain days the Generals decide to issue orders for maneuvers, and the first decision they take is to cordon off the streets. It's been some time since they have shown their faces. They must be waiting for equipment.

Uncle Genari comports himself better than that; he often makes an appearance at the balls organized by the Centre. He regularly dances with a former Opera singer. When he goes home every evening, he stores his white shoes in a box. He is always in an excellent good mood, never a trace of crudeness. We all know that he went to New York as a young man and met a girl with freckles and flaming hair. They say he played the clarinet in some cheerful joint. All the same, when he returned he married the daughter of a well-to-do alderman. The wedding dinner was held in Montcada. The bride, all decked out in blue ribbons, looked quite happy. A few years later, she died in the Aliança Hospital. I was still young at the time, and they wouldn't tell me what she died of.

This is getting very complicated, unnecessarily so. It's actually much simpler than that. Proof lies in the stockbrokers' attitude and character. Their movements are never futile. In contrast, I, for example, show a lack of discretion by ordering a dozen profiteroles. What should I do with them? No one has turned up to eat them; they're in the corner getting moldy. What have I gained? I've learned to put aside pomp and vanity, attitudes that have grown progressively more rachitic. I tell myself it's advisable to stay calm, but I suffer the constant pressure of my instinct urging me to abandon myself to some new, violent adventure, to accept a carefully tendered challenge. In any event, I have to wash my hands first. This will effectively allow me to improvise some novel invitations and prepare myself to dance out onto the terrace.

Ioia will not acquiesce. Unlike many of her companions, she doesn't need a petticoat in order to dance. Considering the short period of time she'll continue to have such fine thighs, she believes it's a waste of time. Wise of her. The problem is, I limp and she can't bend her knees. Not our fault. Our fingers, however, show such delicacy that people admire them when we turn the pages of a book. Moreover, neither of us has heard "In a Persian Market," and we have refrained from embracing girls from Valencia. I must say, my first impression of Ioia was spot on, and in the course of a few days I began adapting to the spiritual rhythm of that household: cheerful in the morning, circumspect at noon, affectionate in the evening. This enabled me to go to bed at night feeling proud that I had not committed any errors. I wasn't sure if my own sentiments were guiding my life or if I just found that particular routine comforting. In the first place, it was Grandmother who was responsible for my sense of intoxication during that time. Need I add that she was an extraordinary person? For example, she always ate her breakfast alone and would send me her greeting of *bon dia* via the gardener. In the evenings after dinner, she played solitaire or, sometimes, when I was in bed, she would ask Rosa to throw the cards and tell her fortune. Grandmother would congratulate Rosa on her cookies or point out tactfully that the bottom of the cake was slightly burnt, but when she did this, she would immediately praise Rosa's daughter, little Elionor, for her beauty: *Yesterday she was but a violet, but today we have a budding rose.* One afternoon, as soon as Grandmother and

I had sat down in the gold parlor overlooking the terrace, the sky blackened, the wind ceased, the frogs grew mute. The figure of the gardener on horseback appeared in the distance through an opening in the lavender field. We spotted him again carrying rakes on his shoulder and rolling a piece of cherry sap as he headed toward the orange trees in the green house. Suddenly, an enormous drop fell on the iron railing that gave onto the fragrant garden with its lingering perfume. Another drop smashed against the shutters, and all at once, as if the sky had gone mad, a terrible downpour commenced. I made as if to close the glazed shutters, but Grandmother stopped me. Seated in the armchair, I felt a shudder, an unfamiliar ecstasy. The hailstorm reached its peak, then a regular rain followed, finally a gentle drizzle. The frogs by the rows of poplar and birch trees began croaking again. The setting sun cast shafts of light on the battlements of the castle ruins and for the last time ignited the transparent leaves that crowned the trees. Grandmother had remained silent throughout, but now she began to speak, at the precise moment I too wished to speak, and in such a perfect tone of voice that I believed no one in this world was comparable to her. How long did we continue talking and listening to the rain on the roof? I only recall that it was impossible for me to sleep that night, and for the first time in my life I saw the sun rise and knew what the dawn was.

Now Ioia is a whole different story. That's why I must always be vigilant and keep a tight rein on the wires that move the sets of this lyrical play. I must be certain that the walls of Nineveh do not appear when it should be the gates to hell. I have to remind myself repeatedly that I cannot pull the strings in a haphazard fashion. Each instant has its own design. And when the director comes to me full of bitter reproaches, I retire to the shelter of my doss, completely despondent. Of course, I could always go visit my cousin. That's the thing to do, go with no sense of guilt, immaculate like her, like the edging on the round tablecloth, like the spools and skeins she keeps in a little basket.

Fortunately, the corner druggist has invited me to a First Communion. He doesn't follow the Bishop's instructions: He has had a very expensive dress made for his daughter. He ignores the miserable people in Asia and America. The women will scream their heads off. The heirs—who already run the businesses—will have burning cheeks and knock over glasses. Only the rich, discerning aunt with the fancy hat will keep her distance. The niece's son will seize a lily and begin to eat it. An angry hand will make him sit down. I myself, who am planning to attend the party with the indecorous purpose of seeking profit, will be exposed mid-banquet. Never again will the druggist look kindly on me. The universe will not be accessible to me now. I will again be the monster who only charts his own insecurity, feeling in his flesh the indifference of those who are closest.

As for the mayor, day after day he increases the number of announcements—exaggerates them—exhorting people to be more ambitious. At first the pedestrians agree, but as soon as they cross the bridge or a seagull flies past, the words become meaningless. Need I point out that the proclamations are directed at himself? He doesn't know why; he just has the vague impression that this is what he should do. He merely repeats that we should be more motivated. Events, though, prove that this is a lie. No one knows what is needed. Even so, the days roll by and each new dawn finds the citizens more nervous, more inclined to make plans. And analyzing the situation only makes the town's daily life more frenetic.

In the meantime, I wait. I take aim at Archangel Saint Gabriel, now that he has returned from speaking with Mohammed behind the dunes. I can't visualize the figure of the Prophet. The Archangel, however, is fluttering above the vertical line of the orchard. I shoot. I know I won't hit him.

Nor will I force the issue. The young girl is standing on the balcony. Her mother wiggles her butt on the sofa and shakes out the damask. The procession is at four. Corpus Christi. Everyone has scattered flowers. Lota would somehow like to devote herself to art or politics. As a matter of fact, she's already conspiring. We could say that in general, there are lots of people who conspire and complain that they are not loved enough. People want to fornicate less and less. It is true you can still encounter some old men who maintain that it's essential to keep yourself well fucked, but they don't practice what they preach and may not even believe it themselves. This is an old notion that reflects the days when it was still popular. Lota doesn't know what she should do; as soon as she rises in the morning she throws herself into three different, contradictory projects. They write about her in the newspaper. Her uncle still holds out hope that her imposture will have some effect: that's why she pretends to be capable of keeping faithfully to a routine which of late has begun to show symptoms of decay. Some days she no longer wears cologne.

I should leave them. Poor but clean: that's a good slogan. To hell with Vienna. And the archangels. And the incubi. Me? I'm heading on my Harley Davidson to the neighborhood of La Sagrera.

When I return, Mireia phones to tell me she believes in God—a little bit—and that she's wearing a pink bra. I told her I didn't plan to budge because my radio didn't work. I don't know what conclusion she drew from that.

The devil dared to attack me this morning. He was only able to injure my thumb. Pleased with my victory, I climbed up on the barstool and read the newspaper. I realize it's offensive, but I often succumb to this temptation and behave like one of those guys selling vegetables at the farmer's market. Despite this, might I reveal that I am waiting, gripped by a twofold hope? Yes: I can confess both to Ioia and to Teia. It's not easy; I have to find the proper venue. With Ioia, for example, it has to be resolved at the Cinema Atlàntic, at eleven o'clock. It's the only place, the only way— despite the fact that she doesn't want to recognize that this is so. I have to deceive her with all manner of distasteful tricks. I have to show up with the neatly folded *Jornal do Renascimento* under my arm, my hair combed straight back.

What can I do this afternoon other than board a train heading south? I don't think I'll go into the center of town. I'll head over, wait on the platform, take a few steps. There's really no need to go, because I don't believe the Battle of the Ebro—like many others— actually took place. The shells and scraps of metal that the jobless collect in the area are pure rust. In any event, if we must rid ourselves of all that land in order to certify this nonexistence, it will require a lot of courage. We have more than enough territory with Tibidabo and a piece of the Collserola Mountains. For years now our most distinguished thinkers have seen the advantages of maintaining a few clear positions.

We just need a name. We should think of one. There was that man who built a house and when it was finished couldn't find a name for it. We can't let this happen to us. It's true that he used to go there, but he needed to get out of town at dawn on Sundays to avoid questions. He was never happy in that house. He dissimulated this fact. Threw parties. Played the violin as he moved up and down the terrace, but the friendships he initiated never worked out. Visits? Only a few drunken foreigners who would vomit all over the rugs. The life of that dedicated citizen was ruined by shame.

I am standing far from those cows. Recumbent cows with warm udders. Brown and white udders. I busy myself reflecting on whether it's good to have a skinny wife. Thin women tend to suffer more discomfort, have sallow faces and frequent backaches. They need to spend long hours lying in a chaise longue. It is true, on the other hand, that some are known to be good cooks, or rather they make good pastries but soon tire of it. In the end they might make a *Braç de gitano*—Gypsy Arm, that rolled sponge cake—once a year, at most. More than anything else, they live and survive thanks to their reputations. Perhaps their art is primarily scenic. If they should happen to marry a guitarist, they might still make something of their lives.

For the time being, the only thing that truly entertains me is the prospect of a business that buys and sells straw. I'll find the energy to rent a warehouse and purchase a long wagon with rubber wheels to transport the bales that clients order. I'll have a strapping lad to help me out. He'll be the one who normally drives the vehicle. I'll take care of the papers, keep tabs on the stock, write letters to farmers. In the meantime, I wait with heavy body and agile feet and appeal to hope. The Generals also seem uneasy. The knife-sharpeners, in contrast, are spreading peace from one end of the square to the other, while remaining true to their genuine animal vocation.

I need to take better care of the skin on the backs of my hands. This soap is drying them out. And it's made from oats grown near the town of Mollet. I compensate for this nuisance by removing the sleep crust from my eyes—as one should, with the pinky on my left hand. I always tremble during the early hours. I can continue by doing my nails. I know that in order to triumph, one must have nails that are cut with purpose. I can wear them like a distinguished professor or like a singer. I need to do more research. There must be other models. The only thing not allowed is to give each nail a different style or to change one's *performance* (to use the English word) weekly. It is the first thing people notice. We all know the importance of this first impression as regards any subsequent progress. No polish, it's not necessary. Clean and well-trimmed. Of course that in itself is not sufficient. You must know how to move your fingers. Know whether to place your hands flat or turned onto the side according to the subject being discussed. Everything will depend on this first visit. I'll place one hand flat, on the glass top that protects the wooden table, and raising the other hand slightly, I'll rub my index finger and thumb together, but without overdoing it. Yes, taking everything into consideration, I think I might go for the professorial model. Color: Ivory. Cut: Roman Arch. That'll go well with the two-corner fold, pearl-white handkerchief that I'll tuck in my left breast pocket. If I decide to go this route, then the blazer will have to be satin, the shoes brown. Legs crossed in order to show off my diamond-shaped rhomboids socks. And the secretary? In the waiting room I'll hand her a bunch of violets that I'll hold at my side. I'll completely ignore the copy girl with the oversleeves. Have to save my energy. Right now, the urgent things are the nails and the violets. And to notify the conspirators not to expect me on Friday. But now that I think of it, an undertaking like that in the Besòs neighborhood is unacceptable. I'll have to return to the workers and leave the violets in the woods. It would be pointless to pick them.

For once, I don't find it necessary to consider this a defeat.

Ioia is skirting the pond dangerously. Teia, however, is standing straighter. With her little silver feet, she's crushing the bean plants. I climb up a telephone pole to observe the two of them. For a moment I am filled with regret; the ill wind of calamity is blowing. It's due to the desire to fill my belly and work up some lather. Of course, I only do this on clear days, after the water has washed the dust from the leaves. But on these days I often confuse trains from two different towns. They are similar, but one goes only as far as Salt, the other to Almeda. I know that one departs early in the day, the other mid-afternoon. As for the rest, it's all the same. Twin factories flank the tracks. The tumbleweed doesn't flaunt a bolder green in one house than in another. Gypsies are reluctant to repair the simple mechanisms on their carts. Even so, this perplexity doesn't absorb me. I can deal with it.

So, why shouldn't I allow myself to play this furtive game? I suppose it's because I've delegated so many responsibilities, including reading the newspaper. He skims the paper, forms a clear idea, knows what is happening. Sometimes he has a pain in his lower stomach, but it goes away. He knows how to take care of himself. He visits the doctor. The pain passes and he forgets about the person who cured him. He reads the newspaper again, with renewed zeal. He often feels a terrible despondency, but he can dissimulate. He suffers for all of us.

And then we have the military paymasters, soldiers with muskets, officers with sabers. Detachments, regiments, command stations, pay sites. Poets have always formed part of the front line, both in the crossfire of battle and in parades. Women have always showered confetti from balconies.

In view of this, perhaps I should buy a treatise on geography: then I would know where I am. I should also visit the monumental mason. People who work with marble are honest. I've always had pleasant dealings with them, especially with the one from Almeda.

But for now, I'm wearing my skullcap, fleeing without the Bishop's permission. I've waited too long for his pastoral. The very Bishop of Rome has often given the impression that he would throw himself down into the Square. That would explain the constant presence of a guard by his side.

Thank God I learned to jerk off when I was young!

Summer 1974
Miquel Bauçà
P.O. Box 9471 (Barcelona)

The Old Man

It was two o'clock in the afternoon. Everyone lay in their regulation beds, tense and alert; eyes and mouths tightly shut, sphincters
contracted to avoid a trip to the water tank, which would have been
a first admission of weakness. A shudder ran through the whole of
the building's population. Someone had just lowered the wooden
blinds with a bang: The new tenant must have arrived. Outside,
the pigeons fluttered away from the cornice and into the dense,
sultry air. Shortly thereafter, from the far end of the street, came
the sputtering rumble of a motorcycle that had been left idling.
The boy talking to the girl from the vegetable stand wasn't the
owner of this contraption. No. The vehicle belonged to the officer
who, on the first Wednesday of every month, climbed the stairs
to give the old man on the first floor a beating. No one flinched,
yet the act had once again drawn attention to the ignominy that
stripped the occupants' lives of any glimmer of brightness. No one
had actually been able to say what the old man's crime had been.
Not even the cleverest matriarch could offer a feasible account. It
was agreed that he had committed some infraction. But when?
What? Had he in the pre-war years allowed his wife to wear black

stockings, folded down over the knee, exposing her naked thighs? On being discovered, had the man been separated from her and confined to the lair where he continues to find shelter today?

This was the explanation that had created an air of conciliation some time ago: a subtle film, a veil that manifested itself through the rugs that could be seen hanging out the windows or across the railings. Suddenly it was no longer necessary to beat the rugs so awkwardly in the dark rooms in back. But, as on other occasions, the illusion was soon dispelled. Had the old man's wife in fact died, been crushed, the very day of her wedding? There was always someone who demanded greater proof, and who would contact the Secretariats to look into the matter or else plead with archivists. But no gratification existed. There was no possibility of casting one's eyes over the serenity of the gods.

I remember that I came to the building in search of a sedative—if not a remedy—for the malady that had befallen me so cruelly some time before. My disquiet was so great that no one could comprehend the depths of the despondency I suffered. No ray of light fell across the shadowy abyss. I had not yet hung up my hat when I heard the sound of rapid panting from the multitude of wretches striding about on the landing upstairs, shoving each other, anxious to drag me into the filth of their own despair. At that moment I didn't stop to consider the extent of what they were communicating. They realized, were offended, and began kicking and spitting. The opportunity to reach an understanding had passed. The fissure that was created would never be overcome. From that moment on, I became merely a contorted shadow, excluded, deaf to their exalted secrets, defenseless, with nothing to keep me from falling into idolatry. Nevertheless, one of the tenants waited for me silently on the landing and tugged at the bottom of my redingote with the hope of discerning my true feelings regarding the old man confined in the building. I could only advise my neighbor to drink from the chalice, to recognize the captive's holiness and flagellate himself at night. In a word, to scream and weep. Frightened by my remarks, he withdrew into the shadows and scurried away to report. I felt ashamed, and yet I could not curse the Almighty.

How was it that I came to this place? The lines of the building had been traced by austere geometers; here the first grandmothers strode quickly about, marching to the same rhythm. The residents' shrieks reached me faintly, barely audible: Only when I ventured into the outer rooms was I forced to listen to their groans and filthy blasphemies. The hammering from across the street—issuing from the owner of a small garage—was no cause for apprehension. He was a happy soul, who worked with his doors open, at times even occupying the pavement. Of course, the man had never been to America, had never felt the need.

I realize now that I erred. I shouldn't let myself be swept away by the comfort of routine. I shouldn't harbor the hope of a new case of incest—not even homicide—which is what the woman who works the cash register at the warehouse does. Anyone could explode in an empty hour and insult the old man as they climb up or down the stairs. When this does occur, the fault never lies with the old man himself. He has never screamed during the routine punishments inflicted on him by the officer. He has never allowed himself to wear cumbersome, tight-fitting clothes, but always loose trousers, always with an elastic band so as not to hamper the functionary's job. Moreover, in the early days he had a dog, but when he realized the animal created an element of perplexity, he didn't hesitate to rid himself of it. He disposed of it so quietly that seven days passed before anyone realized. How did it occur, how did he manage it? The building was again rife with commotion. Grandmothers lost their charm and tore up postcards meant for the niece now living in a land shrouded by fog, married to an alfalfa exporter.

The brothers-in-law were helpless. Having lost their ability to intimidate, they were inclined to produce the liveliest of conjectures instead: The old man had pulled the dog to pieces and flushed these down the drain. This was the most palatable theory until, however, someone suggested they examine the cesspool. No trace of the animal was found. Had the old man managed to swallow the pieces? No one at the assembly dared to insinuate such a thing. Nevertheless, the hypothesis remained active. This constituted yet another wound that would not heal.

The wisdom of that man has never ceased to disturb me. Many times I have had to clench my teeth and resist the temptation to knock on his door. This offensive deed has not yet been consummated. If I dared, I know he would be flattered, but he would feel pressed to betray his well-cloaked secrets, making a gift of their revelation. Then the same thing would happen to me as to all the other newcomers: Sooner or later every one of them moves away. Some cautiously desert, taking with them another gram of wisdom. Others, in contrast, give full rein to their sense of abandonment and depart in plain daylight, tossing their furniture down the stairwell. This causes a tremendous din that they find soothing.

In fact, until now only the woman living closest to the old man has been able to establish the probable hours at which he eats. The smoke coming from his kitchen doesn't provide the clue, but rather the sound of a spoon beating against the edge of a plate. Such a petty method, based upon the belief that this clatter must be cutlery scraping against a dish! But even if this were so, it in no way proves that he is eating at that time. Still, the woman boasts of her expertise and is satisfied with the pretense of homage paid her by the other, obsequious tenants. Even by the rancorous men who on rainy days use the excuse of collecting the laundry on the roof terrace to expose their privates, believing that some fractious young girl will be watching from behind the curtains. On the west side.

Naturally enough, this woman has no female friends or relatives. Women who might have a steady job and laugh when appropriate, or in due course participate in the war by sending parcels to combatants. Combatants about whom only the name is known, not their color, scent, or accent. Female friends or relatives who boldly ride their bicycles through reedbeds and streams to meetings organized in farmsteads by the vicar. No, she was never capable of having any.

Nevertheless, I know this matron will not cause a fire. She keeps her occasional lovers in line, men who with a clumsy gesture might otherwise knock over a lamp. She chooses them carefully, displays them, and they are approved. This is how she can calmly fold the tablecloths and—above all—receive her nephew at any hour of the day when he comes to town to repay a visit. She holds not the slightest doubt concerning the general management of her household. Whence comes this dexterity? Might she have had an uncle, a priest who played the organ on summer evenings with the church doors open so the breeze would dry the parishioners' sweat? An uncle who entertained no suspect affections and therefore spared her curses and lawsuits? An uncle who while young—still far from being sixty, with nicely flat, white hair—had already discovered the warm, straight path? An uncle who, in a word, by looking the other way, allowed the weight of his body to fall away, and so calmed—or so it would seem—the passion of infant-bearing mothers?

Be that as it may, how is it that the tenants don't recognize that the woman is setting them up when she speaks of the old man? Don't they realize that her cerulean cheeks grow taut when she mentions him? Do they know and consent? Most surely. Lacking further evidence, do they cowardly accept the testimonial of the old man's meals, with all the indignity that would imply? Does no one have the courage to accept defeat gracefully? Do they prefer to be sinners and tread on rough, cloddish land far from the pleasant meadows they might otherwise have attained?

This uneasiness penetrates me and defiles me in the depths of my alcove. At this point, I have to buck up and go to market, visit the woman who works with the butcher—though this means I'll return with my basket laden with meat that I will later ingest alone, with no cheerful soul to accompany me.

I could have a falling out with my neighbors, even though they would then immediately adopt a strategy to provoke me further: doors left ajar with women standing in front of mirrors while their most attractive daughters try on stockings. Passing notes and holding eccentric meetings with the purpose of making me scurry about during the forbidden hours.

Nevertheless, can I state that I feel truly forsaken? No. Travelers on the train devote their attention to me: They reflect on my haircut and its part, the size shoe I am wearing. They nod. Only when going through a tunnel does their interest wane and children attempt to violate the rules. But these trajectories are short, and back on the platform everything recommences and no further notice is taken of me. Sometimes there are farmwomen who know where they're going. An excellent decision is to follow one of them who leads us to a broad street, and from there find our way out—without shouting, showing ever greater determination—all the while reminding ourselves that it is *not* a good idea to return to Vienna where conditions are rough; those who risk going there lose their joie de vivre and forget the order of the seasons. The authorities are at the service of people who know where they are. To determine your location, you must first set off, and then continue advancing. The direction is inconsequential. Advance. Could this lead to vicissitudes, cruelties? Of course. Minor ones, but to overcome them you must know how to bend your back elegantly and soldier on. A reward awaits you. It may be clustered together with others, forcing you both to choose and to reject. But the choice shouldn't be difficult, as long as you disregard the criteria of long-haul truckers—criteria that are always much too advanced for our era.

In any event, will it be necessary to abandon the building? The old man can manage without me. He won't suffocate, his head caught between the bars of his cage. He always enters through the door. Nothing forces him to do otherwise.

In the meantime, I could have myself checked out by some saint, a woman who lives in a nearby city. Knowing what my life has in store might calm the turmoil that oppresses me, for clearly I can't continue to do somersaults in bed. When it's time for rest, sleep is short, the dreams harrowing and offensive, forcing me to jump up and raise the blinds again. Would it, however, be beneficial, advantageous, to invest money in this saint? I can wait. It's more feasible, more sensible, to sign up for a coastal cruise. The old legal formalities wouldn't cause trouble—until I actually found myself on the ship's deck. Then the passengers would realize I had come aboard and would insist on their right to sing, dance, and laugh. The captain, though considering it unfair, would be obliged to show me to the gangplank. If, however, I discard these plans, there's always the possibility of marching across open fields, patiently suffering the relevant inclemency. I could move away, in spite of the dust and wind, the beasts that roam the land.

Altogether it's better just to accept the situation without reservation. Not do like those who take Holy Orders believing they will find themselves purged of all vanity when their hour comes, and prefer not to contemplate the future. No one obliges us to follow the path of madness. We can rise above the inclination. We can study in a school that houses a wise man. In other words, the flesh can be beaten down with simple actions, allowing us to devote attention to the mystery, something the old man must do constantly—both inside his cage and out—indifferent to the excitement of the woman who lives next door. She listens, strolls about, and draws certain conclusions; yet in the end she is forced to tell lies. A neighbor who (now that summer is approaching after a rainy spring) won't be able to go to the beach. She knows there's no comparison between her and the girls who appear in the advertisements circulated by the agencies. In contrast, he trembles when the deed requires it of him. Or, if it tickles his fancy, he goes down to the courtyard to sing. He doesn't follow any particular score, he just sings. The matriarchs find this maddening, but for a while they let him be. The order for the singing to cease is usually delivered by the same woman: She pours a bucket of feces on him from high above. The watery excrement falls, hitting the ground. The old man hears the approaching whoosh, but he's never upset by it. He knows the limits beyond which a thing becomes disproportionate. The performance ends, and the old man, fascinated by the silence, returns to darkness. We know that the clamor that occasionally issues from his den doesn't help us to envision anything that's really viable. Like the rest of his neighbors, he too is mortal; so this is not a relevant characteristic. However, the type of trousers he wears is probably significant. Or what he actually eats. Does he weep, and on what days? What if he doesn't groan at all, but bares his chest to misfortune and profanity? And if he were to decide never again to see the light of day, should we take this to mean that he is tormented, consumed by bitterness? It is arduous to explain all this in a meaningful fashion. We will have to settle for vague signs. For example, that he has taken the exact measurements of his room, knows the precise strength of the bars on the window, wears a close-fitting cap like a simple Hungarian Jew and pays attention to his supplies. He constantly replenishes his stocks to avoid venturing out during the calm, ugly hours (traits shared by the building in which he dwells), when he would be forced to have recourse to those exacerbated, peremptory movements that would only benefit the person pursuing him—all the people who besiege him. This caution explains the integrity he has shown until now and the fact that he can today ponder matters and boast that not even in the foulest years of his childhood did he snap a duck's neck as it hid in the reeds.

On the other hand, ambiguities linger: Does he use deodorant, or does he discreetly retain the scent of his own person? And his teeth? What kind of toothbrush does he use? Is he responsible for procuring it? Or did that coarse woman perfumer give him one, making him cringe when he caught a glimpse of it? Does he arrange to have toothbrushes sent to him? Did his uncle bring him some during a visit a few years ago? Either way, it's clear that at some point he reached the conclusion that having white teeth was a prime concern. It's difficult to imagine him being careless about the state of his teeth.

What about love? There are signs that lead us to suppose that he repudiates love. Not that he's exultant about it, as were the meticulous wise men of antiquity—or so they say. Wise men who never ploughed a strip of land and yet were fatigued nonetheless. Who never erected problematic buildings. Savants who didn't travel under the guise of going on a hunt or visiting wives they had dispatched to other regions. Men who never needed to correct these or other errors—nor for that matter were they filled with shame when they faced the mirror. Wise men who, in a word, confirmed what they proclaimed.

The old man—this recluse—is also free from this deceit. Which is why he has never knocked over a vase of flowers, and the potted plant that sits at the end of the sideboard contains just the right amount of earth and fertilizer. As for the hours of the day: Each moment is devoted to the proper activity, as was formerly the case with hermits who so rightly earned their place in heaven, far from the bustling, effervescent crowds of Constantinople, hermits who in the desert had all the sand they wished for their clocks. The news has also reached us that the old man softens the bottoms of his chairs by wisely dividing his time between them. In consonance with this caution, they say his tiles—all of them—preserve the gleam of new ceramics, protected by a thin, even layer of dust. Who among us can boast that we have comparable floors? This is no doubt what galvanizes the matriarchs, who are never satisfied with their own tiles. Necks tense, hands clenched, unable to close their eyes, the women are condemned to the worst possible punishment. How did they come to realize? One of the newcomers . . .

I must refrain from offering further explanations. It's obvious that I can't write to him, though he is a man of letters. Supposing, however, that I were to transgress: I'd be obliged to assume a false name and have the envelopes mailed from port cities so as not to arouse suspicion. I would have to pose as a singer or some other well-established person. No. If one day a review is written about me, it must come through the usual channels. It would calm me if I knew no one else possessed any information as to his origins. Or his education. The world is large. He must be from somewhere. Perhaps one of his ancestors was a horse breeder. Is he aware of this? Probably not. He cast out all genealogical vanity some time ago. His dressers are empty, for he realizes that he is under assault and knows that the final victory will be his. The days pass calmly. As I mentioned, he only goes into the courtyard to sing.

As for me, will I be able to survive him? I'm unable to offer a qualified response. I still can't maintain the regularity of his actions, and I can't move the bucket without its making a grating noise. One must endure, persist, learn. Maybe the other tenants don't suffer the same from life. They don't dare exterminate him: They fear punishment from beyond the grave. This dread causes the matriarchs to remind their husbands—as they set off by bicycle—of the danger incurred when cats jump from the door onto the street. I too can make an effort to garner greater wisdom in other fields. I don't know, for example, the color of the mare that transports the dead in this district. I can own up to my shame and try to find out. Dogs won't bark at me more deliberately because of this. Having this information might offer hope of greater stability. The old man's power derives precisely from this, from possessing legitimate wisdom. The fact that I don't even know how he obtained the privilege of being punished at home shouldn't be cause for discouragement. It must be part of a sinecure position, recognized by some ordinance (which needn't be read). Such information would only lead me to more reflection and perplexity. Better to be resigned and not behave like the drunkards on trains who raise their voices and exclaim about the mistake they made by taking that particular line, all the while on the lookout for the brash soul who will contradict them. The road to kindness is clear. Aside from that, I have to admit that if I were to slip up and pay him a visit, it would only be natural for him to wish to flatter me or ask me to remove the rust from the bars on his cage. I couldn't just sit at a harmonious distance. I'd have to cudgel him, even without a permit and no training. What terrible uneasiness, what remorse I would then feel. What's more, I'm sure my boldness would spread, and then everyone would want to soften him up, till finally the authorities would have to intervene to halt the disturbance and confusion.

I'd better calm down. Now. Bright clouds will appear one day and trigger the desire for a healthy laziness, the yearning to choose the color of one's redingote and politely greet the woman at the vegetable stand. A day that will encourage me to abstain from both great and insignificant wines, and maybe even ignore the agents for a famous vintner—an occupation that must surely attract the attention of any well-established person. Now that the floodgates are open, I could mention that the digestive tract holds no secrets for me. Who among us has never felt a sharp pain in this region? Who, for a reasonable price, wouldn't provide a remedy, a treatment? What can the old man boast of—other than the regularity of his movements? He's much too stiff, like a provincial bloke who reads the gazette religiously. Of course, I shouldn't deceive myself, aside from certain principles. If I, like the rest of the tenants, wish to find peace, it must be by attacking his sense of plenitude. For beginners, I could drop an ingenious smoke-making device down the chimney; few people go up to the roof terrace to hang their clothes for fear of having the quality of their underwear assessed. Now, this explosive would have to be top-quality to assure that it would indeed explode at the end of the trajectory. The generous amount of smoke emitted would have to be sufficiently dense and noxious that the old man could not continue to lie in his thick-barred cage, but would be forced to open his door and window.

At that point, everyone would know if he was a sodomite: One of the newcomers announced that pictures of improperly attired athletes—drenched in their infinite beatitude—hung on one of the old man's walls. Faced with this straightforward explanation, who knows if the tenants wouldn't just opt for lynching him; this would certainly improve our experience in techniques of close intervention. Nevertheless, we should not allow ourselves to expect fulgurations. The building didn't have the proper permits when it was constructed. Every regulation had been broken, and now the occupants were eager to associate the problem with the old man's presence. Formal accusations were filed but never acknowledged. Many buildings are stuck in comparable snags, and there is little municipal land available. In the end, desistance prevails and all actions fade away like dispersing mist.

If you think about it, this old, castigated man never screams, and till now he has never been discovered scribbling on the stairway walls, coining expressions like, "I am not from Samarkand." Nor does he receive visits that could excite the woman who eavesdrops on him, and this makes it more difficult to get raw material to work with. No. When water is scarce or the gas supply is cut, it's for a reasonable reason, one your neighbor can explain. So we improvise. Everyone lends a hand. No one has ever refused. When the time comes, the old man remains immobile, his hands gripping the same two bars, always at the same height. He knows many people use the excuse of all the commotion to place their ears at his keyhole in order to hear him pant. After so many years, however, he can recognize each ear. Depending on whose it is, his grasp tightens. Then he relaxes, opens his eyes, and stares at the light filtering through the chinks of the jalousie blinds, until another tenant stops by and leans against his door. How does he manage not to cough during the disruption? This point has often been discussed during assembly. No one has an answer, but this question disturbs even the most animated of conversations. Men are driven to place their hands at the back of their necks, women to tug at their aprons. Everyone disappears into their den.

As for me, I know soon I will have to make an appearance on one of the landings and have a suitable comment ready. If all goes well, I'll be congratulated, and they'll ask me about my nephew, how his studies are going. That's why I always carry on me a letter from him that confirms his good disposition. To reciprocate, I write my nephew for his Saint's Day, Christmas, and birthday. He has enough money to get by on and is fortunate to have the wife he does. She's hardworking, clean; no one can approach her skill at cooking the quails her cousin sends from his home in the interior of the continent. Still, couldn't this woman take better care of her skin? She says if she can't find top-quality cosmetics, she'll go without. Is it this frankness that keeps her husband in love with her, praising her for it? In any event, I always encourage my nephew to behave in like fashion. Yes. This never-exceeding-the-imperatives-of-the-law helps me overcome the desire to knock on the old man's door. I often think I could pass myself off as someone else, but I've always hesitated, knowing that, nevertheless, I couldn't introduce myself as a simple traveling salesman with his wares. That's clear. I can, nonetheless, picture it. Once I crossed the threshold, I would express interest in the quality of the bars of his cage: test them, find out if they were solid, made of metal, if they were affixed to the floor or put together so that the whole apparatus could be taken apart. It's possible that my interest might make him choke, causing him to weep and tremble like a child. No. I won't do it. The news would spread like wildfire through hallways and corners, and I'd be politely invited to give all manner of explanations. If I had previously made my intentions clear during one of the many assemblies, then I would be able to curb this turmoil. It would be the dawning of a new age. The task of decimating my neighbors would, however, fall to me, with no possibility of a resplendent night . . . Suddenly I put a halt to this frenzy and ask myself: Is this old man truly wise? Perhaps he's only a hunchback who doesn't want to be contemplated by women or bandy-legged youths as he's going down the stairs. Perhaps he was never an attractive young man, one his female cousins would follow with their eyes, and his mother had to intercede—with all the problems this would cause. I know these questions float in the air, awaiting a response, like a crime. It would be a great consolation to know the answer . . . "Does he eat?" asks his neighbor. Who knows what he does! As I mentioned, only a break-in could end his obviously deliberate silence.

I don't have to budge. Plenty of other things obsess me: the reptilian world, igneous rocks, that tediousness that shrivels us up . . . so I was able to restrain myself. In all probability he is *not* a wise man. He was never able to smile modestly at the attorney's office. He didn't refuse to go to Africa on a bloody expedition when it would have been so simple not to sign on. But the promise of incestuous scenes among primitive people caused the firmest of convictions to wane. That's how it was. Today, a drought has laid waste to that continent, and only a few idle volunteers can be found sitting against the wall by the docks.

If some dedicated tenant feels compelled to write up an assessment of the situation, even goes so far as to paste a photo of the old man on my door, I'm sure I'll know to tear the picture up and return to my routine. In preparation, I need to decide once and for all to improve the quality of my sheets; it is my firm intention finally to have silk, seamless sheets manufactured on some island closer to the Orient. I can leave the color to chance, though I know that salmon pink would be the most appropriate—no matter what people who can't afford them might say.

I can afford to go through the daily motions. In the meantime, I occupy my days by making little strips with the fabric that I keep in the trunk, shaping them into balls. Then the children can play with them. Yes. I have room to store them. I'll find the proper moment to distribute them without stirring up envy among all the uncles and brothers-in-law. I'll know how to do it myself. It won't be necessary for a dowser to lend me a hand, someone who has perfected his trade in a village near Constantinople, from whence this art derives its prestige. Despite the confusion, the tradition hasn't been lost. It's not by chance that the Empress Theodoro reigned there. Years later, Charlemagne resumed the practice in a less splendid but more accessible manner. We mustn't forget that during that period, the majority of the population was of barbarian origin. Remote ancestors of General Joffre.

Getting back to the point, the danger doesn't lie with this old man, but with the irresponsible intervention I might occasion if certain circumstances prevail. Keeping my blond mustache nice and tidy could help. If I should be apprehended, I wouldn't be able to go abroad, where train conductors aren't so rigid (they know how to toss their cigarette butts out the window with much greater charm), where peddlers don't shove and garbage collectors dress quite differently. This trip could, however, leave me quite exhausted. And the travelers who risk it, what shape are they in when they return? Anxiety leaves them emaciated and their offspring consumed by vice. No. I'd better resign myself to tolerating the old man. It's only once a month that the guard arrives on his motorcycle . . . Right now, I could dye my eyelashes, something I do with a certain regularity, even though I have recently begun to prefer them in their natural splendor. The secret, as the Book states, is not to go overboard. For millennia—perhaps always—it has been remarked that those who do not pay attention are denied the satisfaction of a life in harmony with seasonal rhythms; they are tormented by an indescribable longing.

Boldly I tell myself that I will not succumb, provided I can resolve certain simple notions, such as knowing if it's necessary to be devout—in the general sense of the word. The most widespread opinion is: no. But nor is the opposite proclaimed. The wounded are proof: They are not killed instantly at the exact kilometer where the accident occurs. People ponder this fact, debate it. We don't know who will have the last word. It's true that we can offer a personal assessment, but that isn't very helpful in settling the matter. It would be a better plan to limit ourselves, reposition ourselves, and propose audible actions. For example: The old man committed some offense and is receiving—at least apparently—his due punishment. We are left with the possibility of becoming overwrought, but sadness always settles in. No. The old man is austere and temperate because he doesn't budge. Has he perhaps achieved a state of weightlessness; does he possess unique faculties that allow him to move from one end of his den to the other without his cage being an obstacle? Can I tolerate the fact that he avails himself of said privileges? It's easy to proclaim benevolence, but also arduous. So, if I rack my brain, what could I use against this old man who is accustomed to beatings? I don't know his deepest convictions. It would be improper to act without knowing them. Besides, one must have agreeable tools, be able to distinguish the weak spots . . . It's not enough to unfurl standards or mobilize the knife-grinders . . . Soon the dearth of all essential materials will be everywhere apparent. Troops are disconcerted; combatants gather round potential leaders who can only affirm their limitations. The plain and the field are there, land suitable for battle, but if one has the opportunity to stand on the top of the mountain, the confusion is perceptible in all of its magnitude. Yes, more convoys filled with ammunition and victuals continue to arrive through the canyon. Yet the siege, the battle, does not commence. The Generals sit in variegated tents from which they emerge so they can be seen sipping coffee. They lend themselves, quite erroneously, to arguments in inappropriate tones. A wind off the foliage sweeps through the camp. The rumor spreads that no program for establishing military merit has been drawn up, nor has anyone given a thought to the box of medals. Sergeants and corporals do not succeed in feigning to agree on the question of conduct, although they were inclined to do so at the onset of the march. This dispute will produce nothing. Perhaps the old man has known more than one contest like this, and that's why he will never be found in a combat situation.

How can one make love on this basis? Only twenty percent of the active population today lend themselves to this communal exercise. This malaise drives many people out onto the streets. It's true that matrons continue to have children, but the number of mothers who send their infants to the provinces as soon as they can speak and walk erect is on the rise. It's not an easy matter to restore the prestige of conscientious fecundity. Few people can offer energetic solutions, and it's pointless to hold on to stale formulas . . . If this were not the case, how many enterprises would be obliged to declare bankruptcy! We are all aware that a factory should be established in an area where raw materials are readily available, where one doesn't always need to be concerned with having an attorney to deal with the resulting lawsuits. If these problems can be solved, the quality of manufactured goods doesn't suffer, and merchandise flows easily into the market. This means that on the site itself, you avoid needing to erect additional buildings. On the other hand, it often happens that the best artisans are found, if not in close proximity, at least within a certain distance. In this case, prosperity increases without causing tension, and one perceives a harmonious integration of the all with the all. Authority becomes unnecessary, which allows mothers to elude taking initiatives that could be dangerous for their children. Mothers can sometimes commit blunders that cause these innocent children to hang themselves by their jacket draw-cords in order to escape scenes of raw anger. Only a few of them survive, resuscitated on the way to the hospital. This is how God punishes mothers who do not believe that He controls the threads of fate. This grave error sends them scurrying in desperation to the fortune-teller.

In any event, we need not pause to consider these inexorable, awkward misfortunes.

Today is Saturday. This is the day the old man rocks himself violently in his cage as the moment of ecstasy grows and multiplies . . . It isn't necessary for me to take an interest in how he enriched himself with such wisdom. I can ignore those who say that he traveled through the Orient, with no relatives to send him letters or munitions; that he escaped ambushes and obstacles thanks to his charm; that when he returned home, in the prime of life, he willingly isolated himself in the most inhospitable barracks filled with depraved soldiers who sodomized him, confusing local customs with regulations; that he could have established himself in a mansion with fine grass, but he accepted the most tedious jobs, in the filthiest areas of the garrison; that he continued to reside there until the authorities drove him out because he was setting a bad example. In short, as one young learned scholar mentioned, the old man enlisted in order to round off the last chapter of his memoirs. If this is the case, it would explain how he gets along so well with the functionary who beats him.

The officer is also a simple man. He lives in a boardinghouse in the suburbs. If you examine him carefully, you'll see that he must have been to Hamburg, perhaps also—at a later date—to Toulouse of Languedoc. That's not certain, though. On Sundays, between nine and twelve, he can be seen at the nearby canteen. He enters, sits, and shrewdly responds to his comrades' observations. He smokes prudently, drinks cautiously, and knows that no one can handcuff criminals with greater expertise than him. He has never boasted of this, however. He walks with a regular stride, consistent and quick, avoiding accelerations that could startle a pensive pedestrian. He doesn't have a dog, or a wife who could phone the radio station to see if he's won the contest. Could he be a clandestine sodomite who has found refuge in this official corps? What establishment could escape slander of this sort from one of its members? In any event, he has never been found in circumstances that would suggest any sort of incontinence upon which a stable theory could be based. Does he steal? Has he stolen? No. Despite many auspicious occasions. As to the job of beating the old man, he undertakes it cheerfully, without viciousness. It's true that when they drew lots, it was his good fortune to be assigned to the old man. His cohorts certainly complain about the men they have to punish instead . . . No. When the officer has fulfilled his obligations, he puts the whip back in its holder, changes his uniform, cranks up his motorcycle, and heads off to sing in a neighborhood choir. He also works hard to keep himself slim, so that he can dress according to the dictates of fashion. As a result, when he goes out onto the boulevard, he doesn't need to be overly obsequious to the attorney who remains seated or to the colonel who leads his regiment . . . No unpleasantness with his landlady, nothing that would seem to stand in contradiction to his general conduct. He gladly allows her to enter his room and inspect the objects hidden at the backs of his drawers; she comes according to an agreed upon calendar—though he would prefer it to be more spontaneous. If the weather is nice, on Saturdays they go out onto the balcony to expose themselves to the requisite curiosity of those who dwell across the street: He stands, knee bent, one hand on the railing; she sits, staring at the kentia palm she has brought outside. If it begins to rain, they stretch and go in. Once again in the living room, they share magazines, intimately satisfied that they can attest to the fact that sin has been kept at bay. They gaze deeply into each other's eyes, unhesitatingly. Vases, gewgaws, and clocks continue in their proper place, immobile, with tiny notes in beautiful script indicating their dates and provenance. Never wishing to burden her (quite the contrary, he is always eager to be a source of respite) he refrains from wearing his fancy leather boots in the house. She appreciates the gesture, brags about him, comparing him advantageously to the dentist, who has never restored the nickel-plating on his drills, nor thought to upholster his chairs. That is why he has the patients he deserves: flatterers who feel compelled to excuse him by stating that his lack of initiative is merely due to his desire to avoid disturbing them. This self-important dentist has never considered buying a new syringe. The officer, in contrast, knows how to eschew groping young girls in yellow sweaters on the bus. This breaks the hearts of the mothers who accompany them. When they reach the end of the bus line, he is warmly congratulated. The officer seizes the moment to examine the buttons on his jacket. He does not glance around in order not to be caught. If someone plays the accordion, he knows the musician and the melody. When he reaches the entrance to his building, he climbs the stairs, opens the door, lies down, and drowses. Nothing can hurt him now.

The Warden

My buttocks are resting on the sheet. I feel the cold against my skin. The murmur of eternity whispers outside.

In the kitchen the warden wiggles her ass. Arrogant. Like the knights who roared through the foam or were scratched by gorse, like the ancient philosophers and hermits, or those opportunistic Sunday fishermen who attacked trains with their riggings, only to be seen shortly thereafter scattered along piers, breakwaters, and crags, in pursuit of the morning salema.

This is the twenty-first day.

The sea must be rough now, rain in the north, wind from the south-southwest. That's the report for the day. You long for confirmation, but part of the forecast will naturally miss its mark. I'll need to keep calm. The waters will become still again and the sea will have ripples, the north will be muddy, the wind will blow in the same direction.

We, the impatient ones, must never resort to spineless cunning, moving ahead, cowardly, wishing only for a change of names. No . . . There are still some—a few remain—who do not lose their bearings, even in pajamas, with one foot resting on a chair and maracas in their hands. What is their secret? This knowledge cannot be learned; it is either hereditary or the fruit of some early instinct. It's best if I just accept it. None of that pointless galloping about. The obstacle is within sight. You can't demolish a wall from a distance, from any distance . . . As to your feet: Learn to untether them. Only then could a glow light up my eyes and create the conditions that would allow me to transcend the illustration in the manual and use a fencing foil properly, cutting figures in the air that would discourage even the most determined assailants. Only then could I confess to a wise man with his hair swept back that it is all one and the same . . . All of this in order to have a well-ventilated home and a touch of crimson on the cheeks that might provoke some sudden infatuations. Assuming that everyone remains in the dark.

Dry mouth. Last night's dreams have left sores in my mouth. My hands are fine. Out on the street, vegetable vendors are at their stands, arms and fingers available. I'll have to do as they wish if I want their embraces to be brief. Otherwise, the same thing will happen to them as to the stockbrokers whose greed provokes such frequent confrontations with the bailiffs . . . The baker and her daughters, in contrast, know how to remove the leftover trash. When they put on their shawls and ring for the elevator, they know precisely what they're doing. They aren't at a loss when the concierge brags that he's been down to the river. Calm and severe, they stare at him, then cross the lobby as a halo—an aureole— follows them as far as the threshold. It's not, of course, this sparse, sporadic, juvenile radiance that moves them, but cultural constants. The hats they sometimes have the pleasure of wearing are not, therefore, an unreasonable caprice. The feathers that adorn them are not always silly plumes that stand straight up: It depends on the color, the dress, the day. And yet, the misses do not pretend to indoctrinate their little cousins. The chiffon and trim that complete their outfits are associated with precise moments in the history of their lineage. The Brandenburgs reflected in their buttonholes might refer judiciously to the moment when the tribal chief gave the order to move on, perching the women on horseback, the children beside them, trusting the presentiment that foretold of open land in a distant place. When the tribe discovered the new territory, they devoted themselves to apiculture. Today, it's an irrefutable fact that the sugar oozing from the figs in the fig tree plantations played an important role. And besides, that splendid vision kept those nomads thrilled for all time.

I jump up. Smooth my eyebrows. The warden concurs from behind the curtains where she continues to stand. Excitement flutters in my gaze, as it did for the ancient light-filled colossi who bathed self-confidently at dawn in the clear river pools.

Shepherds and shepherdesses are again crossing the stream by the moss-covered wooden bridge on their way to the tablelands. In the Beguines' orchard, the bean plants are ready to be harvested. Soon the construction workers will start to file past, rattling their pannikins. At two o'clock, they will offer a toast by the fountain, and a warm, obsessive zephyr will raise occasional ripples in the nearby lake. Banners and a photograph preside over these spirited lads. I take responsibility. The apprentices will let them shout and unwind. This is not the moment to insist on the conspiracy . . . If poplar trees wish to appear whitish, so be it. Who would dare to sully the splendor of the day? Or pester the old nag grazing in the field near the farmhouse? She knows the stable-to-stream trajectory; not troubled by any hazardous decisions, she saunters over to the fence by the apricot trees and observes the lustrous fruit. If I were like the nag, if I acted like her, my teeth wouldn't chatter, and I could propagate myself and fight on different fronts simultaneously . . . Many traveling salesmen and innkeepers don't want this; they spy on me, infatuated—doesn't matter if they're wearing an apron or not. They'll pay for this. They don't realize the carpenter is already preparing their boxes; he has noticed that the green spot is starting to appear on them, just above the orifice. When their wives come down from hanging out the laundry, the women warn them, tell them the news.

What's the warden up to in her pajamas and bathrobe? Has she again fallen into her intermittent, intemperate whisperings? She gets drunk and goes out early in the morning to expose herself to the anger of those tubby boys who, instead of going to school, romp through the pine needles. If you stop to think about it, what else could she do? Associate herself with a portrait painter, ready to wash his shirts if necessary? That business wouldn't last long.

She's removed the fuses now. She stumbles around, groping her way, smudges the drawings. I hold my breath. She has started to beat the eggs in the dark. She always burns the omelet and fills the ergastulum with an acrid, stifling smoke. I have to return to my palliasse. At this point, with an angry look, she phones the mechanic to come and fix her up. It's the guy with the limp; he never charges her. Later, however, it's the warden's turn: She phones and hangs up, again and again, relentlessly. "Hay and barley," she shouts every time she dials, tossing the filthy receiver into the air. Till everything comes to a halt and she draws away, more obstinate than ever, her fingernails blacker. To make amends, she fries scaly sardines . . . She leaves her work unfinished, but in fact, fortune smiles on her. She can't find the time to have a doctor check her hands. When she calms down, she exclaims that everything is urgent and offensive. Her hours are all strung together; that's how she lives. She trusts in the regular rhythm of the decenniums. She knows what's being proclaimed.

This isn't the moment to concern myself with further clarifications. My stomach is taut when I reach the usual site. No misdirection, no traps. I find undisputed glory through these challenges. Searching for every significant frailty, discarding mediocrity. The warden? Is she going to stop me? Some other woman will befriend me. One with a sailboat, unconcerned by the proliferation of means of transportation in the world. A woman without cousins who change their petticoats just for the heck of it, women with no *finish*, breathless cousins who enter a convent that no longer tends to its orchard. But actually, at the back of the garden there's a patch where an old woman—a Beguine—slaves over the Swiss chard. When it thunders, only this nun knows where the tempest is brewing and what to do if it strikes—even if young boys are making a racket on the other side of the wall. Although she has never had a child, she knows the wickedness of these children. This could be referred to as implicit wisdom. And if one discovers tin cans and chaff on the side of the road in summer? The virgin knows that the rains will return and cleanse the gutters. This confidence prompts her to water the little vegetable patch in the corner, prop up the geraniums, and stanch the novices' impulse to commit an outrage against modesty in their wing of the building.

Today is July first.

The warden appears, approaching in the penumbra. She patiently goes about her morning observations. She shakes the curtains, moves the trinkets aside, feels the hinges. Despite the bad weather, I've decided to stay on as a prisoner. I apply myself diligently, so as not to bloody the air available to me. I keep cotton balls in a bag. If a drop falls on me, I can wipe it off. I know how to reset my kneecap . . . I hurry. I could pass myself off as an idle cowherd (or swineherd) who's just happening by to take a look. If I dared, however, my deception would be obvious, and I'd be reported. Changing occupations like that is punished most particularly . . . All of us want to speak one language only. We reluctantly tolerate a variety of accents, as long as this can be agreed upon and is relevant. Extemporaneities were outlawed twenty millennia ago. As a matter of fact, the work of heroes was only ever this.

The warden too prefers it this way. She doesn't want any nonsense; omens should be interpreted by the river. She can't tolerate having the spell broken, like the times she spots me observing snowflakes shattering against the glass. She stands stock-still staring at her watch till I join her . . . The clarinets aren't playing yet, but the assault has grown less intense; she becomes invisible and returns to the darkness of her padded room to rest . . . I risk moving around, between the chairs. I have lost none of my strength or drive or accuracy . . . I leave and return to my bed of clean flock. There will be no more trouble today . . . I'm holding the asphodels, which are at their greenest now. The chestnut trees stand in the distance, shrouded perhaps by the fog off the river . . . When we meet on the landing, the mechanics throw their apothegms at me. My pace slows, and I ponder the scope, tone, circumstance. I thank the men and slip away to a crystalline, inchoate, incorruptible place.

On the other hand, the musical piece is finished, the rehearsals begun. The first performance will be in the autumn. Its brilliance will not blind the young composer, even if the old folks—the regulars—weep and clap from the parterre . . . Let the exegetes get on with their predictions. Let the harpies bite their ears and bleed to death by the lake.

Flagellate myself? I could. The warden applies herself conscientiously. She doesn't mention it; she doesn't clean or dust. That's why she'll outlast me, struggling against custom, mermaid scales, Triton tails, robbers who sweat while hiding in closets. To thwart her I have to keep my hands smoother, if I wish to compare favorably with her son-in-law's teeth and beard. He's a master locksmith, but he's never skimped on time, products, or experimentation in his toilette. So, when he appears on the balcony to finish massaging his cheeks and neck, women stare at him from behind jalousie shutters. He knows it; that's why his wife jerks him back inside. He finishes, doesn't need a second look at himself, leaves . . . The warden yawns and announces that she'll cook chickpeas. Immediately thereafter you hear the sound of the metal blinds . . . Several hours have passed. The warden is cooking the chickpeas. The odor is unmistakable. I won't budge. She'll let the legumes boil. At the turbid hour of noon, she will devour them beneath the cloth lampshade, curlpapers wrapped around wisps of hair . . . An indestructible force protects her from evil. Not even the most ingenious judges have been able to bring her to trial. The court attendants who risk it stumble against brooms and buckets, open dresser drawers, crooked console tables. And they refuse to continue. This happens many times over until the judge grows confused, removes his robe, assumes the garb of the penitent, and wanders aimlessly across rough, uneven land.

I too must be more on my guard. I can't dry my lips on my forearm, like a madman of scant ingenuity and importance. I'll find someone cleverer for a model. At the very least, someone whose father wore striped shirts. This could (in fact it does) establish a link with the future . . . So, is it possible to collapse into a state of disquiet? Who is safe from alienation, even if everything falls into place, is harmoniously negotiated? . . . Those who are born on fertile, loamy soil have wives suitable to the land. Those lacking discernment, they approach, enter the park, and smile at the people who stroll by. And the strollers, knowing their haylofts and silos to be full, are unafraid and respond by offering their hands . . . It has all been written. Reading is sufficient to resolve certain exigencies, such as how to fold the shirt of the deceased after he has been washed and has surrendered his very last soul. In any event, there's always some relative who is familiar with the procedure and steps forward when she notices the confusion. Her rival submits and withdraws to the pantry. The corpse grows more and more pale. Uncle announces he has work to do. Everyone knows that these orphaned uncles fly off the handle easily. Grandmother eyes the dead man and summons the women, who respond: "Mamà?" They gather in a circle, each of them repeating that she was the first to break water . . . This is how it is reported and circulated in the region.

The warden hasn't coughed for days. She said she would pray to the saint this evening . . . Does she really think I haven't had smallpox? That I like the stockings she wears? Other female guards wear similar stockings, finer ones, perhaps with elastic that's easier to wring out. They pay no attention to the knife-grinder, no matter how much he blows his whistle to announce his presence. They hurry past, forceful and arrogant . . . If by chance they receive an invitation, they know how to walk up the gangplank to the ship. And with such assurance and charm! On board, they don't wander the corridors: They know the cabin number and head directly there. Once they reach their destination, they close the door, throw their bags on the pillow, glance at themselves in the mirror, bring out their credit cards and *The Divine Comedy*, and straightaway change their clothes. They know that between them and the atmosphere around them, there's no room for disaccord. They predict nothing; they get along with their relatives. The voyage ends, but the only thing they remember is Italy and—farther away, more delightful still—the Greek nation itself. They aren't troubled by the attention they have devoted to the gourmets who swarmed around them. These scoundrels were full of strange whims, but they weren't well known, nor was the commotion they caused . . . Not surprising that the men bragged that their houses were always up for sale, that they were continually on the move, would go to Tübingen just for a meal. This arrogance stemmed from the men's secret archives. What filth filled these documents, every epigraph! The women weren't aware of this, nor was it their obligation to know . . . There are always some people who will spread idle tales and file lawsuits—whether they're in the right or not. That's why they suffer a cruel death, their bodies sore-infested, the stench driving away even the most pious. If these gastronomes disliked the partridge they were served and sent for the chef, it was merely to impoverish the peasants who'd raised the birds. So why didn't the authorities step in? The epicures bribed the ministers who issued the orders. The supply of small game and plucked birds dwindled, never reaching the marketplace. All that delicious meat that would have reached impecunious households spoiled in warehouses. Wretched men! Covered with pustules, lacking intimacy and innocence, they never knew the dawn.

The warden sniffs her arms. I too can rearrange my hairs. I rise and stand on my pallet. My body doesn't tremble . . . I leave the fauns and sylvans behind. Let them fight it out, clamber up the grape arbor. So what if they have pleasing buttocks? I can also powder mine . . . I hear the sound of horse hooves. I observe the first rays of sun. I spread my still sleepy wings. I find myself in the courtyard. The farm woman, a sorcerer, is tossing millet to the birds. The horrors of last night are but flameless sparks. Drops of dew roll through my hair, dissolving all uncertainty, as they have many times before . . . The white bowl, so nice and round, that I chipped before I realized it was porcelain, rests gently on the slope of the blankets.

Not a single essay on the technology of decomposition . . . Concrete is clearly the material that is most receptive to molding by a press . . . It's possible to intensify vague memories . . . No one ever reached the conclusion that it was impossible to assault the fortress . . . There are rules, even if you were born in a small town. First off, you have to have been wounded: Let it be seen that an arm was lost in battle. Let the starched redingote sleeve hang loose. Enter. Put aside your fear. It's enough if the girl at the telephone glances up and takes an interest. At this point, ascertain what size shoe she wears, if she has an uncle abroad, if she yearns for a canary or else an animal with a larger belly. We must be bold, like campers who raise a tent with four stakes, build a fire where they fry sausages their wives made in their spare time (when they weren't telling fortunes or corresponding via logogriphs with comrades from other, more rigorous fields) . . . Never forget that with summer comes euphoria; this is the season when ants suffer the most because of their young, but streetlights and the delicate perfume of pine needles soothe them. This is when the saint rejects the Books, flinging them against the wardrobe at night. And deeds occur that rhapsodists recount in an orderly fashion. But none remain. Only in Cuba, among the canes. I know they are there. They won't let me lose my way.

If possible, we must somehow ignore the warden when she's aroused, wets the sheets, and has to open the windows, those times when she's too ardent. If I want her to be gentle with me, I'll have to buy her sweets and invite her to the table. If the situation presents itself, make her some jam, wait till noon, and surprise her with it. If she responds, repeat the endeavor with certain variations, until she's exhausted. At that point only can the windows be reopened. Do so with caution and vivacity. And wait. Wait till nightfall, if I really want to lose myself. That's the only approach— other than to inspect the vessels, clean them. Only then will the warden refrain from buying the fishbowl she's been coveting—the one she is hoping to keep on the sideboard. Only then will my murky urine not have to be collected in the bottle that I empty in the fountain on the square.

The sky is about to burst. The chairs, table, and sideboard will serve as a dam. No doubts have come to befuddle me. I have the Books within reach, right beside me . . . I don't yearn for an impossible marriage that would bring me fortune. I don't want to be a factory manager who farms trout and owns a mansion built with stone that has to be imported because the land is pure clay.

Let's forget about the warden. No sobbing, no shoving. The baker—that charming female baker—is standing by the auditorium. I won't know how to act. The bailiff accidentally wounded her; maybe that's why she walks with a crooked neck. It's true that she was never receptive to my solicitude, my solicitous waiting. Nevertheless, the scryer advises me to wear white buskins. If, out of greed, I lose this chick, I'll just have to resign myself to it. Be satisfied with the decrepit, silver-haired warden. But the girl could liberate me from the warden, and then I could move to the farmers' poorhouse, where the wretched are nursed by libidinous daughters-in-law who expose their buttocks as soon as the doctor shuts the door. The girls know what they want: fast pulses that make the frail, incurable inmates pant.

Everything has primed me to savor the present moment, to be alert to the wonder of it; to understand that it is the shampoo—nothing else—that makes hair luxuriant; to observe snowdrifts at the moment of thaw; to know the disposition of the corridors in the alcazar and the customs of those who dwell therein. I know they pause on the landings, at the turning of the stairwell, gasping for breath. If they leave the shutters open, I recognize their hoarse voices when they chance to encounter one another. But, if a glass is broken, you never hear it shatter. There's a rush to cut the cables to the loudspeakers.

The slamming door shatters the calm, the quiet, the comfort of silence. The glass vials continue to tremble. The warden has left without her keys. When she returns—whip at her waist, determined to flog me in the most sensitive spots—she must find me up and about. Only in this case will I be allowed to continue with the tiles, following the design as if I were a musk cat following a scent trail. . . On the other hand, I ask myself: Is it lawful for her to interrupt the severe discipline I submit myself to? Would this explain the growing sense of turmoil she's experiencing? The possibility for exemption or elusion is slim; if a balance can't be maintained during the winter, I won't last until autumn, the season I long for. I won't see the leaves, won't finger the vines, watch the trout leap, or attend the joyful, dignified christenings that farmers celebrate at that time of year . . . No. I have to dismiss this moment of doubt. There are many auspicious signs. For one: The warden has had a manicure—crimson nails that match the rug. Also: The barber who is assigned to me is a neat man of an agreeable age who knows how to add a touch of imagination without disregarding orders. But the surest indication: Blackbirds and merles flutter around the pond. I can disregard the rest of the signs. It could be treacherous.

The warden has returned and locked herself in. This is a well-deserved truce. Later, we will return to our usual combat. It could begin with the saltshaker: I want it closer to me . . . Salt strewn everywhere, growing damp, hard to remove. Far from glorious. No one had foreseen this degree of impotence. The warden is aware of this and furiously yanks the carrot leaves, hides them beneath the kitchen sink, announcing that she'll collect them later. Then she exits the building to wrestle with a woman in the neighborhood . . .

I do as I'm told. I'm not afraid of the wounds I might suffer in the dispute. I'm not a good arbiter, but they teach me. The most arduous moment comes when they sit on the table, silent and sweating, awaiting my decision. Wisdom, however, advises me not to opt for this route. For now, I dampen my lips with my tongue, glance at the ceiling, and, with my hand stretched behind me, toy with the embroidery on the napkin they've left within reach. In the end, I am forced to speak. I smile and invite both women to visit the saint. They ask for time, trying to decide if this is a trap or merely a precaution . . . I lie down on my cot, so as not to be an obstacle in the semi-darkness. The clock has sounded the hours. The warden approaches, stands before me, and unabashedly disrobes and kneels. Straightaway she takes my member in her mouth and with regular vibrations of her uvula draws the surge and swallows. The other woman disappears behind the curtains . . . With a troubled soul, I have to admit that I cannot pass myself off as a connoisseur of Greek dances . . . No opportunity of expressing one's convictions. I'm consigned to these living quarters, and I cannot prove that I am telling the truth. When the constables seize me to place my head to the wheel, they demand spitting, boots in the stomach, hair pulling, pinching. They are men of great rusticity who live in villages on the far side of the dense forests.

Nevertheless, my excellent conduct becomes more and more evident. When I go up to the castle, I carefully scrutinize the processions, the maneuvers of the sappers and grenadiers who trot along the footpaths. If a siren blasts through the loudspeakers, announcing the cardinal's automobile, I approach. This is the opportune moment for boisterous visitors to comprehend the significance of his scarlet-red. The hod carriers thank me. I tell the women—servants and nannies—that they could easily pass for ladies here . . . I know how it should all be framed: by adding the pastel tones of dusk. The shopkeeper now donning his smock couldn't do any of this; he has only a few trump cards with which to establish himself. The ones he exploits in the early hours of morning when men with hooded eyes stumble against the counter, groping around as they replenish their supplies. People who are later embarrassed, but dare not return the goods. Toward eleven o'clock, visitors tend to be coarser and everything becomes opaque.

As I mentioned, I'm lying on flat ground, by the road, accompanied by my warden . . . What I wouldn't give to be near the sea . . . I'd soon find myself compelled to acquire all the accouterments. A folding screen would be the first necessity. Then a fan. Then binoculars to follow the apothecary's widow who lives opposite the bay. And learn the names of the ships that set sail. Altogether, this would require cases, closets, wardrobes. Maybe even a garage where I could park the car I would need for those occasions when I wanted to leave the coast. And wouldn't there be a beautiful damsel in the sand, with an amethyst chiffon scarf lazing across her thigh? It would have to be so: She would lie there, beside the gorse, the Phoenician juniper, and the heather. I would wave and toss pebbles into the water to arouse the lass and announce my presence. Better still, have a kite, though that would be a bit frenetic. The girl could follow the whole length of the string or watch the kite's graceful ascent into the azure sky. She'd have no excuse not to. Such deeds have occurred for millennia, and there's been no sign that any rectification was necessary. As in other cases, it isn't acceptable to take personal considerations into account. If one truly does not wish to participate, it must be made known, boldly, with none of that begging for complicity—an unequivocal sign of bad taste or meanness of spirit. What's the point of discussing Bulgarian gorse or being a certified speleologist? No, far better to let yourself fall straight down, or hazard being struck by that lightning off the mountain escarpment . . . Otherwise, in the end you run the risk—as does the vicar—of speaking ill of the man who built his house on sand, on the delta. The dwelling has been abandoned to the lashing winds. A mistake, true enough, but the owner is now far away, unconcerned by it, relieved of the burden. Of course, it's bad taste to discuss this. No one knows the actual condition of the land when the first foundations of the house were laid. Perhaps it was later that the water company let a stream flow through, causing erosion. The man couldn't fight against this subterfuge. To end it, he would have had to go up to the village, hang out in the café, maybe even marry the clerk's only daughter . . . By dint of his courage, he was finally able to overthrow them and turn his luck around . . . He could blow his nose as loudly as he wished. Nicely coifed, his body disease-free, his character heroic . . . He preferred to establish his family's lineage in some inhospitable land, a family line that would extend his good name with sufficient grace and fervor so that today anyone could follow in his steps.

Everybody works. If they don't play the violin, they drive a car. Perhaps the greatest contrast between them and me resides in our dress: They get the colors right, while I accumulate useless clothes that neither fit nor hang properly . . . It would serve no purpose if I spread false reports, instilling hope like a psychotherapist, always moving around, traveling by steamship . . . The warden has decided that she'll take it upon herself to wreck the nearby factory. The manager, sensing the opportunity to gain personal advantage, will enlist her services. This endeavor will commence when the section head realizes that it is urgent to take a lover because his wife despises him. The warden will step in, thereby saving delays and gratuitous verbiage. So, when the company agents are discovered leaning against the shelf where the ledgers are kept, their veins slit, no one will be accused. She will stagger home, dazed but satisfied . . . Her mother will bolt the door and mutter: "There are evil people out there." I wouldn't know how to tell her that it was her own daughter. It would be so easy to be brave and keep the place tidy! For example: When I'm hungry, I eat, and—true to my rebellious soul—I select whatever foodstuff most appeals to me. Not like others who eat chickpeas that have taken on a spurious color. The brutes gorge themselves on it at the table. I'm consumed with rage and my hernia protrudes, threatening to strangulate. I can't scream. I can only gnaw on the edge of the sheets and listen to the droning sound of impervious ignominy.

I've consulted quite a lot of archiaters, but as soon as they catch sight of me, they become unsettled and excited. Only those who have nurses from Lyons pay me any attention. They probably see some trait in me—a faint shadow—that reminds them of an uncle. A moment of tenderness transpires. I only realize later, when I'm out on the street. But the Lyonnaise certainly picked up on it, and she certainly exclaimed: "Get out of here!" What can I do, other than pocket my hands to stop their irresponsible tremble and plan for my next appointment? This should allow me to reach the waiting room. I know I can't wave my bank book around in there; that would be a confirmation of my bad faith. Confirmation that I was born in the 1930s? It's all the same. Should I keep cool and lucid, like the porcelain factories that still operate and, precisely because of that, monopolize their sector of industry? Shut my eyes and open my mouth, like the warden does when they're drilling on the street? Patiently press forward, inch past, make my way through the crowd? Not that either, seeing as I'm not quite so cautious as my guardian angel.

The warden has been receiving mechanics for three days now. She insists on advance payment. They are quite hurt by this. They buy new clothes. But at dusk they return. The poet Estaci finds himself in a similar situation . . . I can rest. A lot of people write in the gazette.

From my pallet, I catch a glimpse of a rain that I can identify, a rain that dampens the shirts that belong to brawny, overexcited men who come from rough areas. They have abandoned their parents, grandparents, and animals alike, beneath stormy skies. Now they're filling the icebox at the warehouse . . . I organize the retreat in an orderly fashion, despite the fact that loudspeakers are blasting from roofs and balconies . . . Salty land, like Gomorrah! I won't allow myself to recoil, be left stiff. Their arrows will grow limp while still in their bows. They will fall silent. I won't lose my way. I'll reach the broad valley, the valley that is free of sinners. The twilight will be all mine: the ones I still have, the ones to come . . . The warden won't know how to report it. She might lay siege to me. I too can make concessions, diversions, and she'll be forced to review these maneuvers.

While she's consulting, I'll draw up an inventory of other heroic acts
. . . Does she think I don't know the types of cod that are being imported? I can identify the quality, the feel, the thickness of the cuts;
I can tell by their smell where they were fished. I've been to New-
foundland! I couldn't say the same for other goods. For example, silk
scarves. Who really manufactures them? Which designs most trigger
avarice? And why do they have the power to declare, "Such lethargy
today!" Or, "What a jewel!" It's beyond me. Nevertheless, the loops
she continues to make from cheesecloth or rope-yarn don't shackle
me . . . No gaping chasms have opened. Is it perhaps that the hour
has not yet arrived? It's true that I abuse her, but I don't mention this
intending it to sound like some gratifying victory . . . The chink in
my sheets could be narrowed; she's better than me when it comes to
tolerating the cold and stifling convulsions, a hand on her cheek . . .
But the truth is, I know how to stand erect. As for shoes, my choice
is espadrilles. The color? Bright ochre: convenient for slipping down
corridors and watching the wind winnowing away the chaff. Then
following in that same direction. Doesn't matter that it leads to the
spot where orchids are grown, or to a duller place where only convoys of silent warriors pass by, men transporting unused armament
from the barracks to the scrap-iron depot.

I have to stand still now. The bathers on the other side of the
hedge will teach me. Amazing how they keep their composure,
despite the honking horns from urgent admirers! Farther along,
the cavalcade of horsewomen reminds me that nothing comes
without a price . . . As it is, today the excavations at Carthage have
confirmed the authenticity of the travelers' documents; that is: Although infants were sacrificed, it wasn't out of cruelty. The women's

prodigious fertility prompted that immolation . . . Dolphins (who divide their sleep into short spans, their muzzles at the surface of the water) also persuade me to amend my behavior . . . The color of the seamstresses' gloves reflects their anxiety . . . I, on the other hand, whether from avarice or weakness, can never manage to own a simple credit card . . . It's pointless to contemplate the quality of the fog shrouding the bay if I know that government spending is greater than its income and our companies are headed for bankruptcy. Paper money used to be distributed in homogeneous portions, like women's mascara, which allowed them to delay showing their emotions on the train.

The umbilical cord is never what we want it to be. It dries out. Everyone shrinks from the evidence. Our ancestors had to exaggerate their features in paintings. The foremother's freckle takes on an overly pink tone. The heliconist who played at the royal court in Naples can't hide his roguish conduct. Though it was at the very beginning of the industry, we can't just explain this away. It was the period when tenant farmers would go to dances and jingle Louis d'ors in their pockets, when twin sisters would compete at the piano and grandmothers couldn't dry a single tear. There was little the servants could do to guide the lives of those conceived there. Some years later, a more resolute person set things in order . . . You need to understand that Bordeaux is one thing, and what's said about it quite another. The wisest of the Bordelais accept this. They travel to the capital. The others mutter ugly words in the dining room when they eat, and in the bedroom when they recline. Their wives ignore it. They know what men are like. The women put on their shawls and go out on the porch.

From there they catch the last strains of an aria or the rumble of the new neighbor's car. They pause, seal their lips, licentious, and straightaway head to the sea. They can hardly distinguish one day from another. These incautious women can't find the path to unremitting passion, nor do their eyes meet the metallic manners that attract them. They don't keep to the same spot, or heed the trickle that issues from the fountain.

Me? I'm planting seeds, at regular intervals. Let them grow. After a while, select them, harvest them . . . Let them laugh at this. So what if other men turn the earth with tractors and carouse when they head to the village with trailer-loads of vegetables? Ignore them. Who can guarantee they won't be forced to dump their produce into irrigation ditches and be humiliated by this fact? It's rumored they haven't been seen for some time, but that doesn't bother me. Not one bit. So they went fishing and fell in? What if they were seen in a city, gesticulating in a dusty, mud-caked street, shouting like brutes? It was probably true. Yet, nothing could possibly happen that would give me reason for anxiety . . . Blond crickets will continue their constant harmony in the grass. Fear will not cripple me. The somnambulistic hare will not be an omen.

Soon it will be Saint Sebastian's Day. Saint Sebastian, pierced by arrows, suffering the midday sun, indifferent to the commotion erupting from the seamstresses. He is insusceptible to it. The fact that he is international makes this possible. Incomparably so. The women, however, don't dare eat mint jam; and their suitors can't connect the cables to the loudspeakers at the ball.

Irises grow and are blue. I give thanks to the gods. Lifting my noble head, I reposition my hair.

I am aware that the warden is plotting, undulating, pulsating. My fluidity, however, imposes a sense of tranquility and directs her gaze to softer areas . . . The sinister barbarians don't know where the darts are coming from; the confusion paralyzes them . . . I know I can't aspire to behave like the winegrowers of old, who trod between the rows, loading mules with grape-harvesting baskets mounted on either side of the saddle.

I'm not going to be led astray. Like the morning I yielded to the warden's eccentric caprice . . . We left arm-in-arm, but as soon as we encountered the vegetable man, she stopped short, let out a howl, shoved me against the wall, her foot against my stomach, and discharged a string of grievances. Welders roasting sausages were deprived of their fun and began to tremble. Old men slowed their pace. Blood-avid pigeons fluttered nervously around cornices. Would blood be shed, splattered on the cutlets? The warden stood fast. Was she waiting for the cooks to remove their aprons? Had she forgotten the final dramatic effect? In any event, the scene had lasted too long. The spectators calmed down, the pigeons took flight. Only then did she grow flexible and withdraw her foot. The sky darkened and we returned to our penitentiary, like dogs that have been whipped and don't even whimper. Along the way we encountered night gamblers who were indiscriminately selling cows and oxen—even an exiguous herd of mares—to earn a few silver sous. Some did poorly in the gambling den, but who could forget that moment of cheerful company? Their wives, however, were pained. One of the rasher women forgot her manners and was shunned. At the market she could no longer choose the cut of meat she wanted. The other women stood by the butcher as he unloaded on the disgruntled wife the meat that was meant for outsiders. The unfortunate housewife was unaware of this until she tossed it into the frying pan. The splattering, the wild crackling sound that issued forth, confirmed their revenge, and peals of laughter reverberated through the courtyard, interrupting the familiar tediousness of the hour. Her husband—not yet fully recovered—gnawed and tugged on the piece of meat.

The warden, haggard and opulent, has left her cushioned, padded den. In the kitchen, she removes the viscous grease along the edge of the stove with her thumb. Then she slips back into her lair, where she kisses the feet of the seated Christ that she keeps on the corner dresser . . . Her passionate kisses and sparkling, globular eyes can't make me jealous. I'm not planning to offer her any more new figurines.

Outside, people are gesturing near the moat that surrounds the prison walls. They might be employed in a profession I don't recognize. What first struck me as confusion could be simply reserve and penitence. They are the penitent for whom the entrance is barred. Tomorrow, when my head appears through the arrow slit, the gentle wind ruffling my hair, seeing them will encourage me to attend the assembly of these uncouth, dedicated men. They will set traps for me . . . I'll prove to them that I know all the prophets: I'll be shrewd and keep them straight . . . Like mindless flies the men will collide, bump into chairs, grasp the columns . . . I'll be discreet and stare at the skylight. Should they wish to remove me in triumph, I will lower my eyes and refuse . . . In the meantime, the water in the nearby fountain will flow profusely. Swallows will pause to observe the poet as he jumps across the palisade and places his head on the track. The straight-necked engineer nibbling on a sandwich will be unable to avoid hitting him with his train. The gardener watering the red cabbage will suddenly drop his hoe. On the balcony, Grandmother will lose the hair clip that holds her braids in place. Several hours later, the episode will be discussed during clay baths at the hot springs. As for me, what advantage will I derive from all of this? What visible gain? That the dawn will sketch a more glorious arc; that I'll be able to determine, simply by its trajectory, whether it's a partridge or a quail; or be capable, when I have sinned, of heading straight to the willow forest and, taking a switch, lashing my knees and shoulders? Improbable.

It's important to keep your feet on the ground, flat, ready for the march; to establish yourself solidly on the terrain; to put aside memories of the flood; to not be tempted to sweat beside the mechanics—they will never own a mountain chalet. They aren't rigorous enough. They will have to settle for a calendar above the sideboard. End up like little chicks chirping outside, exposed to the pecking of braver chickens. In the event they make it to the Beguines' Poorhouse, the only thing the men will be able to do is soil the sheets, no matter how much they beg and grovel. They will be carried away and left in the wind, uncleansed. Their exposed nostrils turning red. This point—a minor thing—will not appear in the Book of Acts. Not even their sabots (which will not be removed from their decrepit, mortal remains) will encourage people to be pious. They will continue there without the companionship of sons and sons-in-law: The latter are always away on hunting trips—even in fog or ice—beating animals and trampling on planted fields.

The warden still receives them—the mechanics. As if she didn't have enough problems. From now on, I'm going to be more solicitous; I'll take better care of the instruments that characterize us and comfort her. If one of them were to go off, I'd be dragged from the den, with no hope of punishment, abandoned in the dark. I have to examine them carefully . . . Reject the contumacy of following uncertain paths. Nothing comes without a price . . . She knows how to keep the wooden stakes that surround us erect. I respond by striking them . . . Neither of us constructs anything gratuitously, never constructs something that might mislead outsiders—like the postman did when he carried beams and sun-dried bricks up the knoll in front of the village to build an inextricable shambles of a house, all the while awaiting reporters from faraway places. He didn't notice the villagers' growing contempt . . . A reporter arrived . . . "Who says what?" asked the butcher, suddenly dropping her knife; the blade stuck in the wood. The little photographer gave an inquisitive look . . . The parish reiterated . . . Inevitably, the reporter had found the postman's house . . . Disappointed by the filth, he had glanced around . . . The postman made no attempt to apologize . . . The postman grew more and more befuddled, planning new rooms, further contributing to the confusion.

The warden doesn't want anything like that to happen to me . . . I have tools and gauze. A scar is always good for starting a conversation. A way to gain influence, obtain certain advantages. One of these days, she'll come over to my side. So far, I've rejected her insinuations. The sensible thing would be to restore peace between us: let her jingle the keys if she can't help it. And me, I could be quicker with my clothes. They're badly cut and chafe off my hairs—which won't grow back. Take care of my skin: It's turning sallow, an execrable yellow. With these flaws, what can I do other than wear a bathrobe? I could shave, but that would mean I'd have to repeat the procedure, over and over again, every day, and I have no supply of razors, stones, or leather strops. For beginners, I could straighten my hair . . . It's not true that I'm sitting on a powder keg, and if that were the case, it would never explode. Other types of damage occur more frequently: mothers who choose unflattering colors for their daughters to wear, or who name them "Carme" as soon as they're born; stubborn, dreamy-eyed uncles who want to be buried in their own little hamlet where girls still wear live snakes for bracelets; soiling your bathrobe when you put away the bedspreads; my warden's rival getting a tattoo and squandering all her savings.

The warden, enveloped in the penumbra, continues her calculations but refuses to discuss them frankly. She prefers for me to exert myself, strive to elucidate them. She drops hints during the day, vague indications. I apply myself cheerfully to the task, and I can often puzzle them out. The reward is immediate. Right now, however, I'm filled with anxiety: I can't get it wrong more than three times. That would mean I would be depurated according to stipulations. Then what would I do? Wander the corridors begging for a new warden who'd like to chain me up? Women who are proper wardens want attentive prisoners, ones who are at least familiar with the rules of custodial houses. I know—have known—many of those men who roam around, teary-eyed, drenched in sin. It's agonizing to hear them crying out that they would do anything if only the sacred names of their former guards would cease to resonate in their souls. They no longer frighten anyone on the streets.

Dogs don't run away when they smell them coming. As they grow in number, men on motorcycles gather them up, scrub them, and make them sing hymns under the calm baton of an experienced official. The activity ends and the men are dispersed over a radius of one hundred kilometers. The majority, however, succumb to the river, where they finally cease to float and crabs diligently scour their carcasses . . . So, regarding my warden, I shouldn't have my lips too ready. It's always good to improvise. She doesn't pay much attention to the finishing touches. If she doesn't, why should I? . . . I won't commit the worst sin, which isn't even one of the seven. What I need is an enthusiastic mind, no bad moods from reviewing the shape of the continents, no interruptions . . . People far wiser than I have been able to elude both danger and shame. Their effigies can still be seen hanging in cottages and huts: The bouquets of violets deposited beneath them by grateful hands seem very appropriate. Difficult models, but feasible.

Effortlessly, I jump over the enclosure, careful to avoid making obscure gestures that would mark me as an outsider. I leave the master keys behind. We have entered—all of us together—the civilization of risk. Good deeds are not the right approach. It's the effect that counts. We have to maintain the balance between effects and chairs. If this balance were broken, what would we glimpse, other than harrowing dawns, charred logs, dead leaves, end-of-party confetti? . . . Yes, we would march, but no one would know who we were without a clear insignia. We would be despondent, unable to see the mountain. It would undoubtedly be there, but the fog, smoke, and misery would contradict the evidence.

The warden is intimidated. She no longer dares to tense the cord and trip me. Instead, she spreads the word that I am one of the most curious prisoners she has had . . . She doesn't hold me captive. I'm the one with my hand on the rope. She'll leave as soon as it's dark, shamelessly announcing that she's going to take a look around the countryside. Does she think I could possibly imagine her among the shrubs? Lying is such a poor artifice! She won't deny that she's gone beyond the walls. Probably stopped at an inn where grease and soot cover the napkins and blankets, the backs of chairs. I won't tolerate any more deceit. I will be the first to deceive. I'll put on clean socks without her knowing. The soles of my feet will notice. Could she possibly say anything comparable to that? I am blind to nothing . . . I know she has a friend, a woman who's a saint. But where is the saint known? On the outskirts of town, in houses filled with vicious brothers-in-law who never go out. Always seated, legs spread to show off their woolen socks. This saint was canonized, held in higher esteem than she deserves . . . Not even the bay leaf in the stew adds any taste. Both women have to suffer through it, till the warden finally gives in and dozes off. Sundays with the saint are like this. The warden thinks I don't know.

I've endured . . . endured the dust and the grease. I'm rough, austere; I'm aware of it. I understand the enthymemes and litotes, in space. I'm restoring order . . . I know that to build a grape arbor you have to keep the branches neat and not over-harvest . . . just a little each time.

What about fleeing? I could give it a try. Risk everything at Customs . . . First, I would have to decide which customs office; I know they're much more depressing at the border. No one cleans up the strategies and suggestions that passing expats scribble on the plastered walls. I'm not planning to budge. Where else, other than here, could you find an escaped tailor who wanted to hang himself with his measuring tape?

She's put on her straps. She's gone out, all agitated. My step is more aerial, the tiles shinier. I rock for a while, like a free man. Exempt. No need to reread the gazette. I've stopped caring if the saucy woman at the vegetable stand doesn't smile at me. It's the woman at the drug counter who's being more attentive now—encouraging me, I'd say . . . If a general despondency were to settle in, we would still have the swallows. They neither listen nor read; their chests swell and they shriek above the heads of tormented vendors. They don't criticize the unsewn fringes on the cassocks of derelict priests or the vexed scribes who vomit on bedroom pillows.

Wasn't yesterday ephemeral? All day so rapid. Perhaps I haven't known until now how to act with the noble reserve of renowned prisoners. As a matter of fact, that is precisely the case . . . That's why I feel like changing my espadrilles; this will allow me to march more gracefully and visit areas that are dry and shadeless, with no wild beasts that bite, a place where citron trees give off a baneful air that slimes gloryless battles . . . Speaking plainly: Not everything is without thorns, but the criteria could be more refined . . . That's how the baker does it, and she's managed well enough. Like me, she moves within a well-defined geography; her husband's flour-dusted mustache assures that women will choose her bakery . . . The same thing happens to these sterile uncles who won't deprive themselves of anything and endeavor to dress more elegantly every day, to the point of wearing three-piece amethyst suits that go well with their wives' mantillas. The men limp, but their manners of walking sketch out such jovial figures . . . Among themselves, even those mechanics are capable of displaying diaphanous intentions. They no longer bow their heads or shake them. They celebrate the days . . . So, what if one of their grandmothers went mad? Who remembers? Who bothers to criticize it? The woman died, that's all . . . In short, we must remain confident. A lot of people are: They sing in one place, triumph in another; and in the end, their mothers are proud of them. Being of a certain age, these people can respond to any question . . . Me? What can I do other than whip the children till they scream, so that the ensuing silence that descends on the building seems more playful? Race through ravines and rivers again? No. My legs wouldn't lead me there. I'm not wise as I should be . . . I am immobilized by terror if I feel my calves and those other muscles that have become enervated by the alder trees . . . On the other hand, even if guidelines governing parties and dances are quickly implemented, the problems afflicting us won't disappear. No one has yet managed to calm the grimaces of pain. The more tenacious men last until the first light of dawn. It's true that schnapps is poured from carafes down their throats . . . In workrooms, in quarries, apprentices pretend to mutilate themselves by shackling themselves in chains set out for that purpose.

It's begun to rain again. The news accumulates, then dissolves. For example: My warden's only true love was her ski instructor. She keeps saying that the battered guitar I see in the corner is proof of this . . . The important thing is not to walk too fast. Rid yourself of old ailments . . . Isn't iodine, for example, one of those tinctures that's no longer used? The warden believes this. That's why she has devoted herself completely to me and my health. My surly warden has started cleaning up my prison cell and is struggling to render its tools serviceable again. I'll have to respond by doubling my gestures of generosity. I mustn't let vanity blind me . . . The time for picking violets has passed, and for letting a dying snake frighten me—no matter what color it is, how it slithers up, the poison, the hissing. It knows what it has to do. No panic or obsolete behavior . . . Skirts that fly up: she has bewitched them . . . Could she be stopped by the nurse pushing the gurney holding the husband who has no idea where he is? Improbable. The distance between the two women is constant. One gives out a labored pant and sporadic burps; the other sweats under her arms and between her legs, and a thick serosity oozes from her cranium. In short, they both give off a malodorous aura when the climate is hostile.

I'm calming down.

Even so, I should go back to school with all the old men who want to pass the exam, even though the rhetoricians make them suffer for their effort. It's painful to watch them wringing their hands under the desks. They say they won't return, but they gather in front of the classroom. I could accuse the teachers of being indifferent. The judges would believe me. Who knows, maybe even the warden attends . . . She has a stiff neck some days, but that could be from overexerting herself in some obscure act of debauchery. From now on, I must be more on my guard. More deferential, but without getting worked up . . . I won't let myself get stuck. I have manuals, living examples . . . Like these men who lift weights as soon as they wake up. Austere people who keep only one life-size portrait in their bedroom. Clothes: just the minimum. Shirts: one day solid-colored, the next plaid. And when these men are asked if they have tics, they admit it—but only in their souls. They smile and walk past. As for succubi: not a one . . . They brave the frost wearing a simple redingote. At the office, their handwriting is neat, and travelers admire them from the window. If they cough, they do not turn their face.

It's cold again. The sinners are staying out of sight. But I know they are present. They send letters around with orders; they offend me. The afternoon will be unpleasant. The heavy breathing labored . . . Hazelnuts fall by the side of the road. No one will believe I don't feel like gathering them. I can, however, remake my bed . . . I know how to return the warden's blows. Furiously caught up in her perpetual dream, she will have to bite her tongue and recognize my strength . . . She says she dislikes lyrical compositions . . . I sing arias, without warning her. To stop me, she's forced to propose lascivious games on the rug or piano. For each white key played, one button less. Each octave: the cartridge clip, her belt, her camisole, her pumps, or her braiding. She becomes vertiginous. She's accustomed to it. Afterward, my heart brims with suggestions of how to improve myself . . . First thing is the gallbladder. I'm going to the doctor to have it checked. I won't put up with his doing just anything. He realizes that I know the rudiments. The important thing is the first glance: it has to be frank and cordial. He tells me to come in and recommends treatment, both of us sitting in the semi-darkness. If patients interrupt us, he throws them out, down the stairs.

Not even the sun subdues me. I'm standing close to the mastic tree. Obstinate and brave, I ride silky steeds. The enemy drop their glaives the moment they catch sight of me. I command the men to pick them up. They obey and return them to their scabbards . . . For several hours, the arrogant sky keeps its cerulean blue . . . I've managed to persuade the warden not to put down new tiles. Now that she's eating, she doesn't bang the cutlery . . . My felt hat hasn't fallen off . . . The day is racing by, advancing toward me. I toward it. We meet in a strong embrace . . . The warden is preparing for the changing of the guard. Hurriedly, she puts away the tools. Her rival, her substitute, is abrupt and intolerant . . . I've discovered that my warden has been confiding in someone; she's been seen riding with the old man who gesticulates and speaks in apothegms . . . When asked, she doesn't mind revealing where they go. She doesn't burden me with artifice. The elastic clothing she wears—the rubber fabric—allows her to scream loudly, producing a most dramatic effect—or to show a simple, vivacious sign of affection. She must enjoy this. Till now she was content just with having the tiles clean. There has never been a lack of ammonia.

We are enveloped by darkness. It is nighttime. The man moves away from the edge of the bed and goes to turn on the hot water. He combs his hair . . . The baker wakes up. The baker shakes the woman. The woman turns on the radio. "It's two o'clock," the broadcaster announces in an insinuating tone. A few, brief moments pass and the inner patio erupts into shouts of victory. Finally, they have the evidence they need to bring the baker to trial. The guilty party, however, has tried a new gambit and returns to his rival's bed . . . Our days should be less complicated.

We pay attention only to the most disheartening deeds. At night, we shouldn't confuse the animals' screeches, but preserve our skill and dexterity—like the steed and palfrey—which is to say, all beauty and harmony . . . Who could defend us? The typesetter's wife who set fire to the curtains so her husband would have to call the firemen? No. If they can't get along, they should see a lawyer. Everyone tells them to. They ignore it. But one day the fire will spread, and we'll discover a bunch of infants being tossed into the air, as well as helpless cripples who will be consumed by the flames, in front of portraits of relatives . . . The warden herself doesn't waste any time with extemporaneous admirers. She chooses a mechanic who takes her for a ride in his car. The man wants to go pick thyme. She doesn't refuse—unless the day is inconvenient. He agrees. And thus a new world commences.

It is two o'clock in the afternoon, and it is only right that it be so. On the street, drivers are swept away by greed. If I were out there now, the affable, obstinate, basket-laden matriarchs would stop to let me pass. They wouldn't send for the bailiff; he has other ideas in his head and abandons himself to the sensuality of the hour.

I know the warden better every day. The fact is she's a simple person: She sleeps, goes out, washes. Occasionally, she returns with bags of groceries: seasonal fruit that she tastes and leaves to spoil on the kitchen marble. While the fruit is rotting, she remains invisible, restrained in the depths of the velvet, lustrous blackness of her padded den. After a while, she opens the window. Air enters. This is the order I await, the order to prepare myself, to hurry. The flesh grows taut. She moves, relies on metanoia, nibbles at a lock of hair . . . I too remain immobile. Her steady look of fear makes both of us feel freer. I should be afraid of this desire to take risks, such as visiting the singer (even though I know I will have to stand in line with other men who are more experienced admirers). She's in the Orient now . . . I am trying to calm this longing . . . I'm leaving for Vienna . . . Lying here beneath a willow tree I can see boats floating. I run my fingers through the earth; this loamy soil is unique, known quite deservedly for its color and fineness. What concern could trouble me now? A storm at dusk? I'll see the drops of water falling . . . If I think I perceive a pyramid rising before me, rivers braided together, a foaming whale, I'll go talk to the ice-cream man. No reason for me to be afraid of anything.

This afternoon, the idea for a dynamic project will create the momentum we need to reestablish a sense of confidence . . . By then I'll be braver and can subject myself to the baker and her creative fantasies. I'll declare everything. I'll choose the color: I'll reject white. Salmon pink suggests opposing states of mind that succeed each other. Actually, the color evokes an image of myself sailing, playing the harmonica at the stern or starboard side while the captain smokes in his cabin, sheltered from the cold of the day and the hour, the clock affixed to the wood as his sole witness. From there I would observe the ocean—that abyss of water—being traversed by silent fleets and hostile deeds, as messages, dispatches, and reports are being sent (coded and in plaintext) . . . Given the large number of these buildings, collisions and compromising situations are bound to occur, but they are salvaged at the last moment by the felicitous initiative of a subaltern. Naturally, the precise account of the incidences remains confidential. A document—a calque of antiquated models—is sent to the agencies. There aren't enough models to cover all the episodes. Abroad, there is an attempt to dissimulate this inadequacy with urgent parades of bailiffs. This corps of men, however, is composed of dedicated boys who are more interested in the current drivel than a precise analysis of the facts. As it stands, everyone is counting on the photographs to settle the disputes. No one heeds the convulsions of the moment.

The stoppers don't fit the neck of the flasks. They are too loose. Liquid spills out. Clothes are stained. The stains are hard to remove. An alternative—such as lowering your tone of voice and creating a climate of constant buoyancy that would prepare the soul for any undertaking, whether arduous or simple—does not seem feasible. Perhaps it's even inadvisable . . . From the time of the Empire, or even before that, we have trusted in the jolts of destiny . . . This gave rise to a certain character, a lively stride, the body arched forward.

That's what the warden tells me.

So now I know how to escape and attenuate my natural impulses . . . I don't cross land that has no water. I have no desire to travel to Montenegro in search of a region full of scaly mammals, where the rocky, calcareous terrain creates isolated patches of parched vegetation, where bright clearings and blithe rivulets garland the countryside . . . This is often how I feel when I find myself among those tribes: families that don't shout, but belong to a sect that instructs them in their behavior, where the matriarchs thread a needle as soon as they spot a ripped seam. Affable, bonhomous women who neither open businesses nor allow their daughters to marry without a minimum of show of esteem from their sons-in-law. Women who once a year light all the candles, but without inconveniencing the neighboring woman who is posted nearby. When aroused, they lower the blinds as they murmur, "bona nit"; the pleats in the drapes are so deep that the cretonne captures the searing gaze of the woman leaning over the balustrade. For a moment the neighbor postpones her angry outburst, then goes inside and releases a stream of blasphemy sufficient to ignite the dark. She breaks off when she recalls the puffing locomotive that made it difficult to wait on the bench at the train station.

Me? Useless to pretend. The warden always manages to grasp what I most wish to hide, everything that is most profound. When my time comes to pass away, she'll confront me and take pleasure in forbidding me to be deprived of her presence . . . She'll jump from one thing to another, like a cripple who wants to wait on all the tables . . . If I were able to raise my voice, it would be like sabers slicing through a wave. Laugh? Should we laugh convulsively, as if trying to mimic genets or jackals? Better to have a steady laugh, not a sudden snap that might reflect a clear intention . . . What about eyes? What sort of look should we exploit? Glasses are absolutely necessary. But, which kind? At my age, I can't start pestering the oculist. He gets irritated if you're equivocal. Could I perhaps find a more tolerant, benevolent oculist? That would mean having a conversation with the warden . . . I know she's eager to know the state of the world. I'm familiar with the geography of Alaska. The savannah, on the other hand, is a complicated matter . . . I say I don't know, but first I need to divine what it is she's asking . . . Limit myself to polite responses, season them with a joke that averts a possible conflict . . . I could also admit my ignorance outright; this is always a clever, well-accepted recourse. Or, turn the argument around. Not be left in a daze if she smashes the ashtray against the soup tureen. Not mention a trip to the mountains. She knows how to train herself for wickedness . . . She's more attentive than ever, like the butcher who sells horsemeat and keeps his counter and hooks well shined, his apron smooth . . . Apart from the warden, the enemy in the mountains and hills is on the lookout, more powerful every day. But she holds all the trump cards. There is even greater confusion on the plain . . . The wagons, the cavalry, are stuck. The infantry disperses as it splashes through the water. Nevertheless, they wear uniforms in case there's an inspection; they await orders diligently. But they ram flags into the ground without the slightest sense of position. The Generals spend the night in chamois-colored tents, issuing enthusiastic reports. Some of the men are even digging trenches. I can't allow myself to do this. That should be for those born in the vast solitude of the Pampa, where they dig holes in the ground to bury farmers but glance at the horizon before leveling the earth. That's why they're so good with calculations . . . This resilience encourages the indigenous to board huge ships . . . As for me, I have to draw up—and it's sufficient that I do so—an inventory of the roads they have recommended. It's sufficient to have just a stretch of a road. Doesn't matter if it's meant for sheep or beasts of burden . . . The fog settles, obliterating the confines. No need for a safe-conduct. It's improbable that we would need to renounce any responsibilities.

Analogously, I'm called Gilbert, and somehow this name enjoys immunity. The magistrates know this and feign indifference when I'm introduced. An indifference that is not missed by the attentive people who regularly appear at hearings, conveniently setting up chairs on the steps to the Palau de Justícia—the courthouse. When they go to bed in the evening, they feel permeated by history. During their sleep, they classify everything they have learned at court. The following day they can return to their observation point with an open mind.

This is not the case of the warden, who is interested only in the people dwelling in front of her, where the children cry. There is a seldom-seen musician—and not the kind who boasts of having handled bloody goat heads on certain felicitous occasions. He often has indigestion, however, and his burps can be heard from a great distance, all the way down the block. What kind of food are they giving him? Fava beans, lentils, cucumbers, lettuce, and other flatulent dishes . . . If I were him, I would take my spinet and look for a more austere residence.

I too could look for a dark cavern, where the days are brief and the moss is lush, but I relapse into the arms of the woman who restrains me. She fulfills her obligations by dint of her talent and strength. The authorities are not appreciative. If I wanted to be like her, I would have to learn to present my travails in a more straightforward manner. Then I would resemble the saints in the chapel: When the gypsy woman imprecates them, they give her an icy stare, yet in the cool, semi-darkness of evening they abandon their indolence and quit their poses. The female saints are less playful; they never come down from the altarpiece. The next morning, everybody is back in place. Young girls bring them lilies of the valley; mothers light votive candles; grandmothers—if they feel so inclined—sing them villanelles.

So what if the cushion is stuffed with feathers, what's that to me? Why do I beat the eggs with such vehemence? Do I think it will rid me of the extra fat that makes me feel uncomfortable at the swimming pool? Why this illusion that has me believing that if she could only find a darker mascara she would change the concierge's attitude? The warden must be thinking: "Beat the eggs, then lick the bowl, but you need to adjust those madman's eyeglasses of yours . . ." In the kitchen, my chin all greasy, I'm obliged to close the door. That's when she ransacks my belongings: postcards, rosaries, whips. Thank goodness that druggist taught me how to clean myself up, no matter what kind of mess I got myself into . . . Now she's lying there in the pit. I'll never forget her. Let my tribute to her rest here.

Will the warden be patient? Won't my comings and goings overwhelm her? The frenzy builds up: As soon as I climb one step, I search for another. And this frenzy causes me to wear the wrong buskins so often that I have to go to the cobbler (he fought in the war and shows me his scars); it compels me to visit the new druggist and introduce myself as the bleach man; obliges me to commission only full-face photos of myself to hide my nasal hump. Tolerance has its limits.

The plans are thorough, the mechanisms weak. Every Saturday the music from the worshipers across the street reminds me of this fact. Piety and compunction are always present. The only problem is that the quality of the melodies fluctuates according to the subsidies; they have calculated that the organ has to last five years. The faithful do what they can, like all the folks who keep receipts in blue files for the accountant . . . If these devout people visit their hometowns, they make sure it's on a sunny day. And because they display such readiness, train conductors tend to show them deference . . . Apart from that, their homes don't usually catch on fire. If it does occur, they lose everything. Then they move to another village. The new community welcomes them courteously, despite their obvious lack of furnishings and luggage. Their industriousness, however, pays off. The state deducts a certain amount; the insurance company makes up the difference. Since they don't have usufructary rights, nothing is withheld from their salary. So their sons aren't forced to propagate delinquency, and the girls don't have to whore around the market on winter days. Soon the dining room recovers its former splendor, with even a few added touches that make it more cheerful. On assembly days, they are the first to sing, their hearts calm, free of anxiety.

And the warden? What if she's deliberately lying to me? Today she didn't dust the necks of the flasks. An uncle of hers banged on the door early in the morning. I looked her straight in the eyes. He has, however, visited quite a lot of places! He speaks of smoke and grenades. If it was in a battle, which war? Maybe it was just a skirmish. In any case it didn't take place in Avignon, since he doesn't know who its patron saint is. The image appears all over the city: in wood, stone, copper. Maybe it was farther north, a place about which I have not the slightest knowledge of history or botany.

Besides, the warden's cadenced movements as she dodges the chairs in the dark discourage any initiative to learn more. She has no vices, nor does she sit idly when drawing water in her tin can . . . But she remembers my waywardness. Doesn't mind pointing out my failings. Insignificant promptings, that's all she needs. It's enough for me just to crumple some cellophane . . . That's why I fall into her traps, all of them. Ambush after ambush . . . I realize as soon as she lifts her hand to fasten a roller. That means that I shouldn't yield. I've known for some time that she wouldn't tolerate it. Right there, she would push the sofa aside as she pointed to the battlefield. If I didn't participate, she'd call a mechanic, who would get aroused, push his sleeves up, and throw himself into it. Being familiar with previous episodes, it would be useless to bite him. What kind of referee would she be? Wouldn't she take sides? She'd look the other way, just to further her own foul projects . . . Like those rapacious girls who, centuries before, had left the provinces for life at the Court, hoping to participate in the machinations that took place beneath the King's patient eye, a man always on the alert for all of those recurrent conspiracies . . . The musketeers weren't so formidable. They got drunk in taverns, the only thing they knew how to do . . . Whatever it was they lowered with a rope, it proved unreliable . . . The same for those provincial girls named Lola . . . All of this is recent, characteristic of an advanced stage of industrialization.

That's why I have rational motives for not wanting to make any slipshod announcements about my warden. In today's world, who among us has not had a dark past? Those who deny it are immediately betrayed by the wall lamp with its shiny, cast-iron arm. But why even discuss this? . . . Apparently, dogs (so many races, so varied) continue to be accessible. Even pedigree dogs can still be found. Some from Abyssinia itself . . . Bells—not much used anymore, which leads some to doubt that they were ever needed—not only exist, but an avalanche of novel interpretations fills the teletypes. The warden knows it. Grandmothers know it . . . That's why, if some senseless man reflects, opines, and descants, the women don't even make a face or put down their knitting. The women pay attention only to what is essential, such as what happened to the midwife's son. The midwife doesn't utter a word, but when the postman gets drunk, he lets rumors slip, and they spread through the streets and bramble patches . . . Even so, it takes seven days for the spread-legged man's announcement to be accepted.

I'm a prisoner who can't jump over the enclosure, so I can only implore and be contrite . . . If the warden loved me, if her name really was Lola . . . But she always signs it "Assumpta" at the baker's and on her daily reports . . . She never responds to me. She only gives answers over the radio, on different programs. Then she shares her secrets. But I'm not always listening when she does . . . What do they ask her? About the building's hygiene, if she's pleased with me . . . Till now she's always said she was, but without much emphasis or, for that matter, any hint of a doubt. She knows I listen.

If she had any doubts, she knows I wouldn't be able to set priorities. Like when my uncle—my godfather—left his inheritance to his other nephew . . . There was some talk about a woman . . . When I should have been paying attention, I was seen conversing with the vicar, his beard unkempt. And, of course, the rumors flew, the threats. Unmistakable. The nephew quickly began to conspire . . . I'm paying now for my madness. Did I learn from it? No. For I still haven't changed my name. I could go to the courthouse and with a show of confidence demand the application form. But the clerk would see me hesitating at the last moment and lead me to the door . . . So what's the use of saying that I've been to Italy; that I even worked there as a butler; that I encourage the use of toothpaste; that if someone knocks at the door and it's the nun collecting for charity, I tell her to come in without glancing up from the gazette? Far be it for me to draw on any unnecessary partisanship. "Health and fraternity!" is my courteous greeting when she slips away after talking to the women.

The warden continues to be governed by her upright, indomitable character . . . I have to be good, draw upon her wisdom. Who better than she to administer the budget and compose brief, circumstantial letters that go straight to the heart of the administration? If it's cold, I shouldn't complain but see it as an omen, a positive sign that I could become a model prisoner . . . Have this fact recognized by statute . . . If I don't vacillate, I could receive a favorable response any day now . . . If, however, they move me, I won't know how to perform . . . If only some relative had launched me . . . Your first lessons determine how you will proceed . . . You're nervous, but the day of your premiere arrives; the relatives sitting at the back cheer the young artist. The curtain drops—then flattery, tears, embraces. Audacity has been rewarded. The uncles have taken note of all the details and accessories. And, at home again, no one is reticent about the future. The aunts who had predicted the worst are banned that day. If the beginning is thus, there's little room for misfortune.

In any case, this is the model. The straight path lies ahead . . . If Satan appears, I can banish him immediately. And advance. If he pretends he is not there, be doubly cautious. The devil zigzags around from place to place . . . He can also assume the shape of a man who sweats and wipes away the perspiration . . . I know what he wants, though he might appear to be staring into the depths of the lake. I know bewilderment grips him when he bites his fingernails . . . Not even the perfumed muslin veils at Sunday Mass could make me reconsider these important points! . . . Even if I wander into the scrubland, I'll pretend to know my way. I'll continue till I'm out of his reach. If I encounter a hunter lying in wait with his net and whistle, I'll greet him without being intimate . . . I stand now far above the level of the lake. I pause. I glance at the calm surface of the water. I attempt to extract a secret from it. I glance into the distance, toward the opposite shore where gypsies have set up camp. They have built a fire and are bathing the children.

The warden positions herself beside the door, whip in the air, keys hanging at her hip. I won't have the courage to greet her. There's no guarantee that I won't stumble when I walk by. If I fell, she'd glance up at her assistant, who would pull on the rope. The alarm would spread confusion up and down, down and up . . . None of that smashing of porcelain, none of that making myself bleed so that blood drips across my temples as I stand before the mirror without even that touch of pity that is so useful for orienting yourself . . . Better if I think about the man who says he's shackled by many chains but thinks he will soon be released. Who could believe him? Who could love him? . . . Some time ago there was a reason for passion. The incidents took place at infrequent intervals, but the distance between the account of it and her involvement was so great . . . Yes, we embraced, but passersby noticed the chill. They would stop for a moment, verify the sham, and continue on to their destination . . . What else can I say about the condemned man? That he was run over and has taken up martial arts to help him recover? It might be a lie. It is true that a woman warden was assigned to him, same as me . . . No possibility of deception here. If you are so maladroit as to yield to deceit, you will never recover a sense of peace. That man I mentioned: better if he sacrifices himself—his neck on the kitchen marble—as soon as he arrives. That's the only way order can be reestablished . . . He won't do it. He will, however, take off his blazer and stomp on it, but only after he has sent for witnesses. Then he'll grab the one flowerpot from its ring on the balcony and throw it onto the street. Just to be able to take the broom and dustpan downstairs, stop the cars, and clean up the mess amid the commotion . . . After that, he won't be able to address me, not a word, or start new conversations that might have helped him.

The days pass. I know what the coming ones will be like. I can tell by how the warden lowers the blinds or the air shaft resonates . . . I can't visit the baker today. Her father discovered her—cold and stiff, in her blue pajamas. I'll have to find another woman, coarser perhaps, more distant. I'll have to go to the funeral. The project she had with her husband for urbanization of the scrubland has been abandoned . . . What's the wretched man going to do now? I can't help him; he was my rival. He'll pine away. They'll find him sitting on the stairs . . . Their only words will be: "He's from the third floor; we'll leave him there." I won't be able to do him justice unless I see him being lifted and removed.

But the greyhounds are racing again this afternoon. After they've burned the baker's dresses, if I'm shrewd this evening, I'll be able to find that button among the ashes of the bonfire. When I come back, I'll scrub my body to keep the skin taut. Not like the baker, who will start to shrivel now . . . Can't neglect the knuckles and other joints. What else can frighten me? Nothing really . . . Trains will leave and the sober-minded switchmen won't be sorry. Cooks will stir the casserole without offending and won't pester the help with frivolous orders . . . Placid masons will lay bricks. Ne'er-do-wells will not break windows. Everyone will avoid the ravages of precipitous love. No one will rely on intrigue in order to obtain a position. On the mountains, snow will cover the grime . . . There's a lot of work to be done, a lot of places to visit. Several rosebushes await me . . . Not even the deceased baker—having freely corrupted herself—will accuse me with that (appropriate) stench . . . Young blondes will shake their hair back and comb it. Other girls—the ones with short hair—will also occupy their time.

One must be able to distinguish the crème de la crème . . . The warden has only one skirt, which she washes on Mondays; she doesn't care to have more . . . She follows the example of health-resort managers: When the time comes to do their bookkeeping, they celebrate the season's profits by inviting back the prelates who have been most receptive and supportive. These managers don't stick their necks out for anyone . . . The mountain range hasn't moved . . . Hot water still flows from the springs.

Children don't doodle from the very beginning. No, they learn, day by day, to move the chalk . . . Slowly but surely, the cabbages swell beneath the botanists' looks of disbelief. That the thistle or poppies are perhaps too close doesn't distract the wise men . . . The slave girl who arrived from Friesland gently breathes in the splendid air of the cirque. Then, with a cloth she dusts her master's bust. When he returns from the woods, he reciprocates her kind gesture by cleaning his shoes. I too have written down tasks in the notebook I keep in my pocket, even though I see the warden sharpening one of her husband's straight razors—in case I should wish to escape . . . She also wants to offend me, using the mechanics who line up in the street and the vestibule of the building. She usually chooses one at dusk. The guys are worn out, but return day after day with circles under their eyes, ready to give it another try. She lets them know that that's not what it's about . . . One even dares to bring along a cheap gem, but his hands tremble . . . God will certainly punish her. Nevertheless, she never disconcerts me . . . It's like the guy who asks for salmon, absolutely has to have it. He'd like to offend me too. But I know these animals well, their migratory habits, that soft pink color. Their vivacious movements in the river can be explained either by the fact that the paths of the moon and sun intersect or because the water level's gone down. Fishermen know this and are patient.

I do the same with her. It would help me if I knew whose daughter she was. An anonymous traveling salesman's? A disgraced, degenerate laborer's who lives in a distant, fog-shrouded city where he has started life anew, to such a point that he now goes out and makes rice dishes with the widow with whom he shares a miserable life? Yes, they go out. If the day is icy, however, they eat at home and go to bed early, though at times he sits on the edge of the bed in the dark, his arms crossed. He doesn't see the angel with the flaming sword who's on the point of destroying him because he hasn't reconciled himself to the designs of nature . . . In this foreign city, on these leaden days, girls sew selvage, priests cough and cover their mouths, constables do not patrol, lightning does not flash, the shutters are closed.

If the warden doesn't throw me out, I might still be able to bear this. Where else could I find the intimacy, excitement, and welcome that she offers me? She doesn't tell real-life stories; she leans against the secretary and continues writing in her diary. That's why she's able to go out, plod through the scrubland, and ignore the latest ambush. I respond by not feeling obliged to gnaw on bark; the cave and the grotto are always present. I know how to wound those who are in a hurry to have me removed.

So her skin's oily? It may just appear to be. Another woman might have legs that are too thin, or hair too curly . . . If I choose, it would be enough just to keep my eyes trained on the reeds and frogs that decorate the damask she's hung on the wall . . . If the siege is well coordinated, the intention honest, there's no need for further consideration . . . An elderly person should smile and travel. Come home at night, rock for a while, and look at the clock that sits on the table. Many do just this and discover the advantages, people who never have to chase gondoliers. They leave that to their daughters, who glance out of the corner of their eyes and can actually appreciate the stink of Venice. They aren't impressed by the ride, the port, the dashing man who suddenly appears. That's why they always carry a perfumed handkerchief.

No need to be sad. Let the warden phone, scream, lose herself in all the shouts and gasps from the men who unload flour and bran at the market. We'll see who laughs last. Who says retreat? I'd end up like the man who doesn't know if he should sell bags of hazelnuts in the shell, or the wretched men at the warehouse who work the pulleys in front of the clerk who scrutinizes them from his glass doghouse ... Nobody calls me indolent—I'll prove that I'm diligent. Of course, I could make more of an effort to throw off this lethargy and visit a place that has vetches I can touch: black, round, ripe ... But, what if I just stick to playing the spinet? No one could reproach me, as long as I did it with spirit, without letting my trousers knock against its case.

The warden is all languid now, asleep in her clean clothes. If she doesn't have more changes of clothes, it's because she hasn't yet received compensation. But she knows how to be assertive. It's worth recognizing that before coming here she was stationed in still more depressed areas, had even frailer prisoners. One day she moved north, and here she is today, by my side. I need to be convenient to her, inside the bedroom and out. Confide in her during rest periods, tell her my plans. There's only one way and that's to show myself with generous teeth, even if she shrinks from me or moves elusively in the darkness of her padded alcove. If she bumps into me, she might slap me. This won't happen, because I know the traps and distances; and her heavy breathing is noticeable, whether she's leaning against the sideboard or embracing her crucifix. I know how many steps she takes. It has to do with the number of chairs used as a barrier. On my first day I was told they were my safeguard: She would never jump over them. I'm not afraid that I might hear a truck coming, threatening to remove them. At night, I sometimes think I hear the vehicle in my dreams, but an implacable calm returns with daybreak. I go down to the garden, call to the little niece, put her in the swing in the pergola, and drowse in the grass, my soul all spongy. Quite the opposite of the bishop, who is consumed by doubt, doesn't clean the muck from his ears and isn't appointed to a metropolitan diocese—not even an archdiocese. He lives with a female cousin, and the entire set of china they use is of uncertain origin. The girl reproaches him and has catalogues sent from Limoges. The simplest thing would be for him to have someone set the place on fire. There would be some discussion, a price would be agreed upon, and after the results were evaluated, he would pay the remainder of the stipulated amount. And there'd be no more talk about it. Should he later happen to encounter the perpetrator, they wouldn't know each other. The only problem would be if there were plagiarists and this led to an investigation. If you're contrite, there's nothing to fear. Some scoundrel could say he suspected something, but none of his arguments would stand up. The perplexity this might cause would be eroded over time.

No need to insist on reading and learning from prestigious manuals. Any prepubescent can judge competently. Maybe he would be a bit more reticent, have a different way of expressing himself. So what? You have to be able to evaluate the importance of a frank, spontaneous exposition, executed with no preparation. For example: The farmers who first glimpsed the tree from Japan that produced a golden fruit the size of a walnut immediately thought of a loquat, and together they decided to call it a Japanese loquat. All confusion disappeared. The rest of the farmers, mothers, and children could relax, without fearing in their hearts that the fathers were headed for a bloody brawl . . . None of that unhealthy voluptuosity. No clashes between mother-in-law and daughter-in-law. Each in her own bed, attentive only to the passing hours marked by the clock on the wall.

Not like the man who borrows supplies and spices from me and doesn't realize that the days pass. If I mentioned it to him, he'd show his gratitude by offering me serenades, nocturnes and aubades. All of it quite over the top. When he has turkeys, he feeds them so much that the birds have trouble clucking. He could follow the example of the locksmiths he hears all through the day: They've never attempted to mimic the raucous cry of an animal, not even the sound of the conch shell at the fishmonger's . . . Or like the tragedian living upstairs, who neither accelerates nor abandons but stomps his cothurni on the floor, day after day, until finally he reaches his plenitude, that plenitude that oozes through the cracks and spreads.

I've been happy for too many days now. I'm afraid my guts might burst . . . Now I can allow the sweat to trickle calmly down me. I can feel my occiput without bragging about it, as the Aeolic warriors did before mooring their ships. And not without reason: The story of their heroic deeds is still alive today . . . I shouldn't blame myself for not taking part in trendier activities, like the old fellows who dance on Sundays and even arrange the garlands, tinsel, and oriflammes. Always on the lookout, their canes tapping, eager for new news, renewed news. As for their wives, they too remember that this is the season for red cabbage, green peas, cucumber, leaks, onions and garlics, cassava and cauliflower. These old men refuse to take medicine but can often be found in the mountains, applauding spontaneous groups of singers. If they should happen to pass away, they've always managed to shut their eyes first, and are suffused by the warm freshness of their bedrooms. Their habitual cleanliness means that once they're stiff it isn't difficult to wash them. Their cohorts point this out on a sign in the Day Center . . . What should I do about the fact that they are so near? Reschedule my commitments, practice compunction, heighten my silence, avoid being knifed by a guy from the Philippines. These last fellows definitely know how to talk, and the girls love to hear Tagalog. Certain languages are privileged. This theory continues to be valid. Can eloquence be useful to us? Yes. Always. Provided it's framed by effect. The giants of remote times—wise men according to everyone's estimation—were mute by nature. That's why they lived longer. Speaking shortens our lives.

The warden is also silent. I am too. Till now she's had no reason for complaint. There are few prisoners like me. Your run-of-the-mill convict immediately joins a gang, riots, demands to be moved to another cellblock just so the cleaning women will have to work longer hours. That's a mistake. Once these women have finished braiding their hair and carefully studied the exits, they can sneak tools to the men. I shun this kind of behavior, and this allows me to measure the distances and establish true relationships. Self-denial is my sole companion. What would I gain by signing up, adding my name to other lists? . . . Here in the dark, I know the warden is vigilant. Her warm, frantic breath reaches me, ready for combat. She's lying down now. I can risk slipping past her. My fingers are agile. I know how to push the chairs aside. She always aligns them in such a way that she can identify the exact direction in which I'm moving and I won't be thrown off course but only more exposed. It's my turn to respond. I'll put on my espadrilles: they cushion my feet, quicken my stride, are conducive to rest . . . Repair the damaged parts. Use more and more toothpaste . . . Would eagles and skate fish have excelled if they hadn't been so determined and courageous in their attempts to recognize air and water currents? . . . Masters from other areas warn us of the baneful snare of melancholy. Here it would be better, if it were possible, for grandmothers to stop pursuing their granddaughters, for singers not to want a house near the casino. Who goes there anyway? Clients with little self-control, who then have to sleep in their cars, parked in an unpaved, sodded alleyway. Irresponsible clients who don't realize they are contributing to the scourge of unemployment among the locals . . . Even though fishmongers get splattered and use their knuckles to wipe the smudges from their eyes, these women know the incalculable consequences of this terrible situation. That's why they're careful how they spend their money. Gradually they stop giving their nieces presents. No one feels hurt, and the example spreads: The little cousin who wanted to go abroad decides to marry the apothecary; the brothers-in-law drop their lawsuits.

I redeem myself as well. Even if I appear more audacious, there will be no playing of flageolets—those symbols of a forgotten past. What could these instruments contribute to modern people? In any event, nothing decisive that could persuade us to discard forever the memory of the Roman plough and look bravely into the future. These are the facts, though doors may squeak, curtains won't close, the plaster is damp, and my fingertips tremble (because an organist caught them in the keys or because the old man sleeping atop the water tank fell off).

The days pass. Mornings are urgently repeated. I don't follow meteoroidal changes carefully enough. I continue on my way; no indictment docket can frighten me . . . The catalogues are old, no longer used. Continents are not moving at the rate we would like. Pubescent boys still do somersaults. Magistrates debate the extent of the penalty they will hand down to the little client with a cough. My hair is no longer curly. I don't wear new three-piece suits any more, and the geraniums in the tiny garden openly incriminate me because of this. My feline stride is filled with insignificance when I trudge from my cot to the toilet. I no longer learn from wounded children, strapped in their strollers, playing with a ball. Nor do I search for a stone to finish killing the rat on the edge of the road, trampled because it was unaware of the danger of wandering astray . . . I can, however, convince myself that these practices are unusual. If this is possible, then the words will be truthful and I will prevail . . . They will beat the warden across the brow, and she'll find it hard to pluck her eyebrows. When evening comes, I'll be able to tell myself that I've salvaged the day and did not fall into disgrace. No need for additional insurance. If I soil my hands, I have the wherewithal to correct the situation. And I will sing. This will be the point around which barricades of strength will be erected in ever-growing concentric circles . . . I can't forget, however, that the shopkeeper selling cruets could break my momentum simply by stepping back. No use turning to stare at the flour vendor. She's closed.

Tomorrow is Thursday.

The warden shouldn't have told me. The mane I would like to stroke (with no alarming gestures, no foolish incongruities) is outside . . . No, it's not that . . . The stale odor of a mattress—the smell that drove me to commit illustrious, audacious deeds when I was young—doesn't reach me now. Other men in other places tremble and are misled, but they can neither travel around nor stray from the musical score. They go to dances where the soloist puts his heart into the music, but the lyrics don't suit the place, and, naturally, this affects the men. They don't quite weep, because they know they are among stern people who stroll about with daggers at their waists and scarves decorated with ships and seagulls tied around their necks. This is what the premises call for. They know that when the soloist leaves, the new manager will use the place only for weddings, without realizing that the tendency is toward simpler weddings held in the mountains . . . This type of discomfort used to be a familiar thing. Today, the manager is unable to anticipate new trends . . . If I should move, there will be no grueling contest, even if genuine mastiffs do race up the incline so the unruly sheep won't roll down and drown.

Time doesn't exist for the Fates. They continue to spin in the loft of the new temple. Covered with mildew, they sit in damp chairs, ignored even by the owls. Things are not what they used to be. Before, when the flesh of the deceased had fallen away, the healthy bones were braided together, the rest thrown to the dogs.

How should I prepare for my escape? It's not enough to have the tools. The right moment must come. And then I will have to jump on the nag that is tethered to the ring in the wall. Above all, no matter what happens, seek simplicity and grandeur. Guard against the unexpected: Every moment is precious when it comes to checking the sutures . . . Never mind that Uncle rules that the damp walls are the result of skimping on cement . . . The fact remains: When the warden smiled at me, I couldn't do a somersault. She, however, responded with a splendid gesture. I had forgotten that when someone straightens their hair, smiles, and immediately takes a graceful step, you shouldn't hesitate.

She hasn't locked me up, but I feel certain she'd be willing to gouge my eye out with a fingernail. If I can remain still, she won't, but she will deliberately shove the dish with her elbow. I'll pretend that I'm mending the bits of pottery . . . Has my hour come? What will I do at that moment? Will I be able to refrain from murmuring,

"The seagulls are flying past?" Will I hold my stomach so it doesn't growl and give me away? If I had a rope with a hook, I could throw it over the wall, test it, and begin scaling. But I might be left hanging there, and the benevolent admiration of children and mothers would turn to shocking derision. Nevertheless, it must be done. The crucial week is approaching; my permission to stay here is almost up. She could grant me an extension—if she wanted to. But she'll prefer to replace me with another prisoner, one who is more inept, more impertinent. It isn't easy to find a prisoner like me, one who has survived the great snowstorms. If I manage to escape, I'll know to seize hold of the heather. I'll move from one plant to another until I finally reach the sands. Here I will encounter my veritable end, the definitive, equivocal caress. There is no other road. The climates will be diverse, the assaults abrupt. I will have to reconcile myself to this . . . The Fates hold tiny skeins. Nevertheless, wells of pleasant water do exist, though I know I can only approach them with a spongy soul, clean teeth, and perfectly-parted hair. The wells hold the waters from a succession of eternal dews.

The time with my warden is drawing to a close. Soon I'll be far away. I'll wear my rubber shoes in anticipation of what is to come. May God guide me and care for me. May the endeavor provide me with memorable moments . . . I'm in no mood for any hodge-podge . . . I still hold a few trump cards . . . There will be no more wars. Officers and troops will coexist peacefully. Will I be able to rise to the occasion and confront this new era? The saints await me, restless and jovial. I must reach my destination.

Barcelona, 1988

CATALAN LITERATURE SERIES

The Catalan Literature Series at Dalkey Archive Press presents modern classics of Catalan fiction in English translation, featuring exceptional authors at the forefront of Catalan letters. The Series aims to bring English-language readers closer to one of Europe's oldest, yet still relatively unknown bodies of literature, with a history stretching from medieval times to the present day, thanks to Catalan authors' persistent belief in the power of literature to express the complexity of individual and cultural identity.

The series is published in cooperation with the Institut Ramon Llull (www.llull.cat), a public consortium responsible for the promotion of Catalan language and culture abroad.

MIQUEL BAUÇÀ (1940–2005) was perhaps the most radical stylist, iconoclast, and visionary in Catalan literature: eschewing publicity, insulting his peers, and writing unclassifiable books. Today he is seen as a cult figure, and his works as contemporary classics.

MARTHA TENNENT, a translator from Catalan and Spanish, was born in the United States, but has lived most of her life in Barcelona, receiving her BA and PhD in English from the University of Barcelona. She is the editor of *Training for the New Millennium: Pedagogies for Translation and Interpreting*, and recently translated the novels *Death in Spring* by Mercè Rodoreda, *The Invisible City* by Emili Rosales, and *The Violin of Auschwitz* by Maria Àngels Anglada. Her latest translation, the *Selected Stories* of Mercè Rodoreda, received a grant from the National Endowment for the Arts.

SELECTED DALKEY ARCHIVE TITLES

PETROS ABATZOGLOU, *What Does Mrs. Freeman Want?*
MICHAL AJVAZ, *The Golden Age.*
The Other City.
PIERRE ALBERT-BIROT, *Grabinoulor.*
YUZ ALESHKOVSKY, *Kangaroo.*
FELIPE ALFAU, *Chromos.*
Locos.
JOÃO ALMINO, *The Book of Emotions.*
IVAN ÂNGELO, *The Celebration.*
The Tower of Glass.
DAVID ANTIN, *Talking.*
ANTÓNIO LOBO ANTUNES, *Knowledge of Hell.*
The Splendor of Portugal.
ALAIN ARIAS-MISSON, *Theatre of Incest.*
IFTIKHAR ARIF AND WAQAS KHWAJA, EDS., *Modern Poetry of Pakistan.*
JOHN ASHBERY AND JAMES SCHUYLER, *A Nest of Ninnies.*
ROBERT ASHLEY, *Perfect Lives.*
GABRIELA AVIGUR-ROTEM, *Heatwave and Crazy Birds.*
HEIMRAD BÄCKER, *transcript.*
DJUNA BARNES, *Ladies Almanack.*
Ryder.
JOHN BARTH, *LETTERS.*
Sabbatical.
DONALD BARTHELME, *The King.*
Paradise.
SVETISLAV BASARA, *Chinese Letter.*
MIQUEL BAUÇÀ, *The Siege in the Room.*
RENÉ BELLETTO, *Dying.*
MAREK BIEŃCZYK, *Transparency.*
MARK BINELLI, *Sacco and Vanzetti Must Die!*
ANDREI BITOV, *Pushkin House.*
ANDREJ BLATNIK, *You Do Understand.*
LOUIS PAUL BOON, *Chapel Road.*
My Little War.
Summer in Termuren.
ROGER BOYLAN, *Killoyle.*
IGNÁCIO DE LOYOLA BRANDÃO, *Anonymous Celebrity.*
The Good-Bye Angel.
Teeth under the Sun.
Zero.
BONNIE BREMSER, *Troia: Mexican Memoirs.*
CHRISTINE BROOKE-ROSE, *Amalgamemnon.*
BRIGID BROPHY, *In Transit.*
MEREDITH BROSNAN, *Mr. Dynamite.*
GERALD L. BRUNS, *Modern Poetry and the Idea of Language.*
EVGENY BUNIMOVICH AND J. KATES, EDS., *Contemporary Russian Poetry: An Anthology.*
GABRIELLE BURTON, *Heartbreak Hotel.*
MICHEL BUTOR, *Degrees.*
Mobile.
Portrait of the Artist as a Young Ape.
G. CABRERA INFANTE, *Infante's Inferno.*
Three Trapped Tigers.
JULIETA CAMPOS, *The Fear of Losing Eurydice.*
ANNE CARSON, *Eros the Bittersweet.*
ORLY CASTEL-BLOOM, *Dolly City.*
CAMILO JOSÉ CELA, *Christ versus Arizona.*
The Family of Pascual Duarte.
The Hive.
LOUIS-FERDINAND CÉLINE, *Castle to Castle.*
Conversations with Professor Y.
London Bridge.

Normance.
North.
Rigadoon.
MARIE CHAIX, *The Laurels of Lake Constance.*
HUGO CHARTERIS, *The Tide Is Right.*
JEROME CHARYN, *The Tar Baby.*
ERIC CHEVILLARD, *Demolishing Nisard.*
LUIS CHITARRONI, *The No Variations.*
MARC CHOLODENKO, *Mordechai Schamz.*
JOSHUA COHEN, *Witz.*
EMILY HOLMES COLEMAN, *The Shutter of Snow.*
ROBERT COOVER, *A Night at the Movies.*
STANLEY CRAWFORD, *Log of the S.S. The Mrs Unguentine.*
Some Instructions to My Wife.
ROBERT CREELEY, *Collected Prose.*
RENÉ CREVEL, *Putting My Foot in It.*
RALPH CUSACK, *Cadenza.*
SUSAN DAITCH, *L.C.*
Storytown.
NICHOLAS DELBANCO, *The Count of Concord.*
Sherbrookes.
NIGEL DENNIS, *Cards of Identity.*
PETER DIMOCK, *A Short Rhetoric for Leaving the Family.*
ARIEL DORFMAN, *Konfidenz.*
COLEMAN DOWELL, *The Houses of Children.*
Island People.
Too Much Flesh and Jabez.
ARKADII DRAGOMOSHCHENKO, *Dust.*
RIKKI DUCORNET, *The Complete Butcher's Tales.*
The Fountains of Neptune.
The Jade Cabinet.
The One Marvelous Thing.
Phosphor in Dreamland.
The Stain.
The Word "Desire."
WILLIAM EASTLAKE, *The Bamboo Bed.*
Castle Keep.
Lyric of the Circle Heart.
JEAN ECHENOZ, *Chopin's Move.*
STANLEY ELKIN, *A Bad Man.*
Boswell: A Modern Comedy.
Criers and Kibitzers, Kibitzers and Criers.
The Dick Gibson Show.
The Franchiser.
George Mills.
The Living End.
The MacGuffin.
The Magic Kingdom.
Mrs. Ted Bliss.
The Rabbi of Lud.
Van Gogh's Room at Arles.
FRANÇOIS EMMANUEL, *Invitation to a Voyage.*
ANNIE ERNAUX, *Cleaned Out.*
SALVADOR ESPRIU, *Ariadne in the Grotesque Labyrinth.*
LAUREN FAIRBANKS, *Muzzle Thyself.*
Sister Carrie.
LESLIE A. FIEDLER, *Love and Death in the American Novel.*
JUAN FILLOY, *Faction.*
Op Oloop.
ANDY FITCH, *Pop Poetics.*
GUSTAVE FLAUBERT, *Bouvard and Pécuchet.*
KASS FLEISHER, *Talking out of School.*

FOR A FULL LIST OF PUBLICATIONS, VISIT:
www.dalkeyarchive.com

SELECTED DALKEY ARCHIVE TITLES

FORD MADOX FORD,
  The March of Literature.
JON FOSSE, *Aliss at the Fire.*
  Melancholy.
MAX FRISCH, *I'm Not Stiller.*
  Man in the Holocene.
CARLOS FUENTES, *Christopher Unborn.*
  Distant Relations.
  Terra Nostra.
  Vlad.
  Where the Air Is Clear.
TAKEHIKO FUKUNAGA, *Flowers of Grass.*
WILLIAM GADDIS, *J R.*
  The Recognitions.
JANICE GALLOWAY, *Foreign Parts.*
  The Trick Is to Keep Breathing.
WILLIAM H. GASS, *Cartesian Sonata
  and Other Novellas.*
  Finding a Form.
  A Temple of Texts.
  The Tunnel.
  Willie Masters' Lonesome Wife.
GÉRARD GAVARRY, *Hoppla! 1 2 3.*
  Making a Novel.
ETIENNE GILSON,
  The Arts of the Beautiful.
  Forms and Substances in the Arts.
C. S. GISCOMBE, *Giscome Road.*
  Here.
  Prairie Style.
DOUGLAS GLOVER, *Bad News of the Heart.*
  The Enamoured Knight.
WITOLD GOMBROWICZ,
  A Kind of Testament.
PAULO EMÍLIO SALES GOMES, *P's Three
  Women.*
KAREN ELIZABETH GORDON, *The Red Shoes.*
GEORGI GOSPODINOV, *Natural Novel.*
JUAN GOYTISOLO, *Count Julian.*
  Exiled from Almost Everywhere.
  Juan the Landless.
  Makbara.
  Marks of Identity.
PATRICK GRAINVILLE, *The Cave of Heaven.*
HENRY GREEN, *Back.*
  Blindness.
  Concluding.
  Doting.
  Nothing.
JACK GREEN, *Fire the Bastards!*
JIŘÍ GRUŠA, *The Questionnaire.*
GABRIEL GUDDING,
  Rhode Island Notebook.
MELA HARTWIG, *Am I a Redundant
  Human Being?*
JOHN HAWKES, *The Passion Artist.*
  Whistlejacket.
ELIZABETH HEIGHWAY, ED., *Contemporary
  Georgian Fiction.*
ALEKSANDAR HEMON, ED.,
  Best European Fiction.
AIDAN HIGGINS, *Balcony of Europe.*
  A Bestiary.
  Blind Man's Bluff
  Bornholm Night-Ferry.
  Darkling Plain: Texts for the Air.
  Flotsam and Jetsam.
  Langrishe, Go Down.
  Scenes from a Receding Past.
  Windy Arbours.
KEIZO HINO, *Isle of Dreams.*
KAZUSHI HOSAKA, *Plainsong.*

ALDOUS HUXLEY, *Antic Hay.*
  Crome Yellow.
  Point Counter Point.
  Those Barren Leaves.
  Time Must Have a Stop.
NAOYUKI II, *The Shadow of a Blue Cat.*
MIKHAIL IOSSEL AND JEFF PARKER, EDS.,
  *Amerika: Russian Writers View the
  United States.*
DRAGO JANČAR, *The Galley Slave.*
GERT JONKE, *The Distant Sound.*
  Geometric Regional Novel.
  Homage to Czerny.
  The System of Vienna.
JACQUES JOUET, *Mountain R.*
  Savage.
  Upstaged.
CHARLES JULIET, *Conversations with
  Samuel Beckett and Bram van
  Velde.*
MIEKO KANAI, *The Word Book.*
YORAM KANIUK, *Life on Sandpaper.*
HUGH KENNER, *The Counterfeiters.*
  *Flaubert, Joyce and Beckett:
  The Stoic Comedians.*
  Joyce's Voices.
DANILO KIŠ, *The Attic.*
  Garden, Ashes.
  The Lute and the Scars
  Psalm 44.
  A Tomb for Boris Davidovich.
ANITA KONKKA, *A Fool's Paradise.*
GEORGE KONRÁD, *The City Builder.*
TADEUSZ KONWICKI, *A Minor Apocalypse.*
  The Polish Complex.
MENIS KOUMANDAREAS, *Koula.*
ELAINE KRAF, *The Princess of 72nd Street.*
JIM KRUSOE, *Iceland.*
AYŞE KULIN, *Farewell: A Mansion in
  Occupied Istanbul.*
EWA KURYLUK, *Century 21.*
EMILIO LASCANO TEGUI, *On Elegance
  While Sleeping.*
ERIC LAURRENT, *Do Not Touch.*
HERVÉ LE TELLIER, *The Sextine Chapel.*
  *A Thousand Pearls (for a Thousand
  Pennies)*
VIOLETTE LEDUC, *La Bâtarde.*
EDOUARD LEVÉ, *Autoportrait.*
  Suicide.
MARIO LEVI, *Istanbul Was a Fairy Tale.*
SUZANNE JILL LEVINE, *The Subversive
  Scribe: Translating Latin
  American Fiction.*
DEBORAH LEVY, *Billy and Girl.*
  *Pillow Talk in Europe and Other
  Places.*
JOSÉ LEZAMA LIMA, *Paradiso.*
ROSA LIKSOM, *Dark Paradise.*
OSMAN LINS, *Avalovara.*
  The Queen of the Prisons of Greece.
ALF MAC LOCHLAINN,
  The Corpus in the Library.
  Out of Focus.
RON LOEWINSOHN, *Magnetic Field(s).*
MINA LOY, *Stories and Essays of Mina Loy.*
BRIAN LYNCH, *The Winner of Sorrow.*
D. KEITH MANO, *Take Five.*
MICHELINE AHARONIAN MARCOM,
  The Mirror in the Well.
BEN MARCUS,
  The Age of Wire and String.

WALLACE MARKFIELD,
Teitlebaum's Window.
To an Early Grave.
DAVID MARKSON, *Reader's Block.*
Springer's Progress.
Wittgenstein's Mistress.
CAROLE MASO, *AVA.*
LADISLAV MATEJKA AND KRYSTYNA
POMORSKA, EDS.,
Readings in Russian Poetics:
Formalist and Structuralist Views.
HARRY MATHEWS,
The Case of the Persevering Maltese:
Collected Essays.
Cigarettes.
The Conversions.
The Human Country: New and
Collected Stories.
The Journalist.
My Life in CIA.
Singular Pleasures.
The Sinking of the Odradek
Stadium.
Tlooth.
20 Lines a Day.
JOSEPH MCELROY,
Night Soul and Other Stories.
THOMAS MCGONIGLE,
Going to Patchogue.
ROBERT L. MCLAUGHLIN, ED., *Innovations:*
An Anthology of Modern &
Contemporary Fiction.
ABDELWAHAB MEDDEB, *Talismano.*
GERHARD MEIER, *Isle of the Dead.*
HERMAN MELVILLE, *The Confidence-Man.*
AMANDA MICHALOPOULOU, *I'd Like.*
STEVEN MILLHAUSER, *The Barnum Museum.*
In the Penny Arcade.
RALPH J. MILLS, JR., *Essays on Poetry.*
MOMUS, *The Book of Jokes.*
CHRISTINE MONTALBETTI, *The Origin of Man.*
Western.
OLIVE MOORE, *Spleen.*
NICHOLAS MOSLEY, *Accident.*
Assassins.
Catastrophe Practice.
Children of Darkness and Light.
Experience and Religion.
A Garden of Trees.
God's Hazard.
The Hesperides Tree.
Hopeful Monsters.
Imago Bird.
Impossible Object.
Inventing God.
Judith.
Look at the Dark.
Natalie Natalia.
Paradoxes of Peace.
Serpent.
Time at War.
The Uses of Slime Mould:
Essays of Four Decades.
WARREN MOTTE,
Fables of the Novel: French Fiction
since 1990.
Fiction Now: The French Novel in
the 21st Century.
Oulipo: A Primer of Potential
Literature.
GERALD MURNANE, *Barley Patch.*
Inland.

YVES NAVARRE, *Our Share of Time.*
Sweet Tooth.
DOROTHY NELSON, *In Night's City.*
Tar and Feathers.
ESHKOL NEVO, *Homesick.*
WILFRIDO D. NOLLEDO, *But for the Lovers.*
FLANN O'BRIEN, *At Swim-Two-Birds.*
At War.
The Best of Myles.
The Dalkey Archive.
Further Cuttings.
The Hard Life.
The Poor Mouth.
The Third Policeman.
CLAUDE OLLIER, *The Mise-en-Scène.*
Wert and the Life Without End.
GIOVANNI ORELLI, *Walaschek's Dream.*
PATRIK OUŘEDNÍK, *Europeana.*
The Opportune Moment, 1855.
BORIS PAHOR, *Necropolis.*
FERNANDO DEL PASO, *News from the Empire.*
Palinuro of Mexico.
ROBERT PINGET, *The Inquisitory.*
Mahu or The Material.
Trio.
A. G. PORTA, *The No World Concerto.*
MANUEL PUIG, *Betrayed by Rita Hayworth.*
The Buenos Aires Affair.
Heartbreak Tango.
RAYMOND QUENEAU, *The Last Days.*
Odile.
Pierrot Mon Ami.
Saint Glinglin.
ANN QUIN, *Berg.*
Passages.
Three.
Tripticks.
ISHMAEL REED, *The Free-Lance Pallbearers.*
The Last Days of Louisiana Red.
Ishmael Reed: The Plays.
Juice!
Reckless Eyeballing.
The Terrible Threes.
The Terrible Twos.
Yellow Back Radio Broke-Down.
JASIA REICHARDT, *15 Journeys Warsaw*
to London.
NOËLLE REVAZ, *With the Animals.*
JOÃO UBALDO RIBEIRO, *House of the*
Fortunate Buddhas.
JEAN RICARDOU, *Place Names.*
RAINER MARIA RILKE, *The Notebooks of*
Malte Laurids Brigge.
JULIÁN RÍOS, *The House of Ulysses.*
Larva: A Midsummer Night's Babel.
Poundemonium.
Procession of Shadows.
AUGUSTO ROA BASTOS, *I the Supreme.*
DANIËL ROBBERECHTS, *Arriving in Avignon.*
JEAN ROLIN, *The Explosion of the*
Radiator Hose.
OLIVIER ROLIN, *Hotel Crystal.*
ALIX CLEO ROUBAUD, *Alix's Journal.*
JACQUES ROUBAUD, *The Form of a*
City Changes Faster, Alas, Than
the Human Heart.
The Great Fire of London.
Hortense in Exile.
Hortense Is Abducted.
The Loop.
Mathematics:
The Plurality of Worlds of Lewis.

SELECTED DALKEY ARCHIVE TITLES

FOR A FULL LIST OF PUBLICATIONS, VISIT:
www.dalkeyarchive.com